NAKEYA CHANEY

My Soul to Take

"Vengeance Has No Mercy"

Trigger Warning:

The following content contains depictions of rape, murder, blood, gore, and profanity. Reader discretion is advised. If you find these topics distressing or triggering, please consider skipping this material or accessing it with caution. Take care of yourself and seek support if needed.

Please remember that trigger warnings are intended to provide individuals with the opportunity to make informed choices about what content they engage with, particularly if they have experienced trauma related to the topics mentioned.

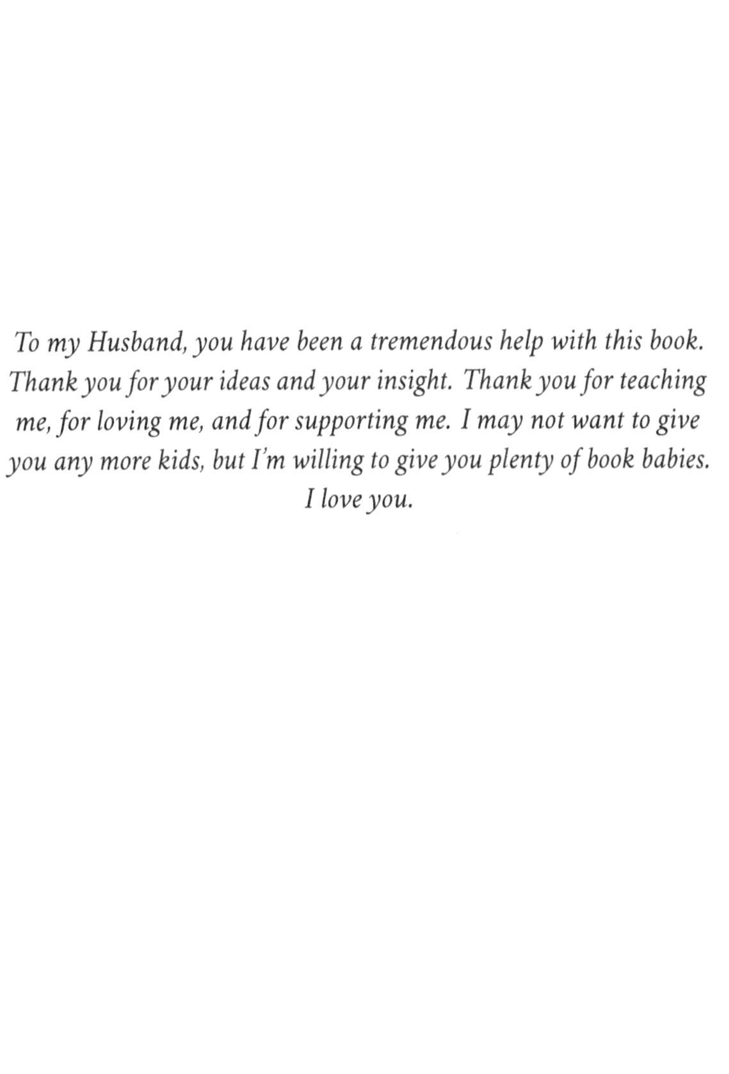

To my Husband, you have been a tremendous help with this book. Thank you for your ideas and your insight. Thank you for teaching me, for loving me, and for supporting me. I may not want to give you any more kids, but I'm willing to give you plenty of book babies. I love you.

Contents

Acknowledgement

To my Daughter, everything I do is for you. Although you are not old enough to read this book, or read at all since you're only three, I want you to know how much I love you. I want you to know that I think of you in everything I do. Thank you for simply being my child.

Trigger Warning:

The following content contains depictions of rape, murder, blood, gore, and profanity. Reader discretion is advised. If you find these topics distressing or triggering, please consider skipping this material or accessing it with caution. Take care of yourself and seek support if needed.

Please remember that trigger warnings are intended to provide individuals with the opportunity to make informed choices about what content they engage with, particularly if they have experienced trauma related to the topics mentioned.

Chapter 1: Demon

I could hear the waves crashing against the rocks on the outside of this dark cave. The cool, salty breeze rushed through the cave's opening. It was cold and inky, but that was just the way I preferred it to be. I knew it was time and could feel it in my body. My depleted energy levels required replenishment.

I looked down at my fingers and toes, which were pale and wrinkled like I had been soaking in a bathtub for hours. However, I have not taken a bath in days. Especially not in this body. I mean, I know the old man I killed already had wrinkled skin, but now that his skin and my skin are decaying, the wrinkles are even more prominent. I need to find a new body.

I pulled myself up into a standing position and wobbled over to the entrance of the cave. It was still dark out, as it must have been around midnight or one in the morning. Everyone should still be asleep, peacefully, in their beds with their families.

I struggled to walk because of my lack of strength. I leaned up against the firm surface of the wall for support. It was foggy out, but even through the fog, I could still see the lights of Claireville illuminating. Stupid people with their flashy lights and nice cars. If only they knew someone like me was lurking in the dark while they were asleep.

I hate people. That is why I enjoy doing what I do. Ever since the fire that took away my humanity, I have had such an urge for vengeance. I was supposed to die that night, but I didn't. However, it would have been easier if I did.

I positioned the skin of my wrist between my incisors and took a deep bite. Slurping the warm blood oozing from the laceration, I began chewing my flesh — his flesh. I took in a deep inhale, savoring every moment of my small feast. This man's blood tastes like trash, but it should grant me enough energy to make it to my next target. I might as well enjoy this old heap of garbage.

With fresh blood smeared across my face, I stumbled out of the cave, which quickly turned into an erect, postured walk. The small amount of energy I needed finally kicked in, and I was on my way to slither into someone else's body.

I was hunting for another identity, another life. Preferably someone who doesn't matter. I would enjoy being a woman this time, maybe even a young woman. I miss being able to heal quickly, but those bodies are hard to get. You rarely see them lying around recklessly. The easy targets are the homeless people. Someone sleeping in their car in an alley or an empty parking lot. Maybe a truck driver who failed to lock and secure their doors. Someone not paying attention. That way I could slip in and slit their throat in the blink of an eye.

As I crept along the shore side, I could smell burning grease from the thick clouds of smoke being pumped into the environment. *Do they not realize we are breathing this shit?* I remember when I used to eat that crap. When I get the body that I want, I refuse to fill it with that rubbish food. Grease, cholesterol, heart attack, in that order. I'm going to treat it as a temple and I know exactly what, who, I want.

I was getting close to my stop, and I could feel it. My lips curled in a creepy, killer fashion. Blood surging through my veins. Adrenaline heightened, ready to slice the throat of my next victim.

Keeping away from the city lights, I slithered through the darkness to the countryside. A nice little area where screams go unnoticed. Just the way I like it.

Chapter 2: Demon

I reached the mouth of a long dirt road. The trees forming a canopy over the trail, creating a creepy and unsettling ambiance. The moon emits sufficient light for me to see a few feet within my view. Ample light makes it easier to notice this road leads to a residential home, judging by the mailbox with a house number attached to the side of it.

I pursued my journey down the unfamiliar but familiar road. The area seems different because it is dark but also, the mapping from Google maps was dated years ago. I checked my pockets to confirm the presence of my handy, pre-filled syringe and to ensure my favorite pocket-knife was within reach.

My palms are sweaty because of the anticipation I'm getting from knowing I'll be able to slice and dice in a few. I pulled the knife out of my pocket and ran my fingers across the piercing blade. Splitting open the superficial skin to anchor me in reality, placing me in the current moment. Crimson seeping down the blade, hinging off the tip before splattering onto the ground.

A few yards away sat an old brick home. The photos from the Google map displayed this home in pristine condition. It's now withered away like an old lady whose youth-filled years have long passed. Now, someone has boarded up the windows and the shutters are lopsided. This home looks like it was waiting for someone shady like me to show up. "Well honey, I'm here." I say aloud, twirling my wrist in a circular motion.

I reach the steps of the house and to the front door. I took a moment to crack my neck and wiggle my extremities to provide full range of motion. Given this old fart's body being infested with arthritis and gout, I'm going to need the extra ability.

As I twist the knob, it doesn't surprise me to find that the door unlocked. There's not a damn thing in here worth stealing. It smells like mothballs, corn chips, and cigarettes. It's dark, but the moonlight shining through the cracks in the boards on the windows illuminates the thick cloud sitting still in the air. It's evident that there is no airflow in this house. Just hot, stale, funk.

I have been snatching bodies for so long that being quiet is something that comes second nature to me. Granted, I may be an old guy now, but in a few minutes, I will be a 34-year-old woman. I can't wait. Melissa Gardner doesn't do drugs, that's if you don't count her anti-depressant medications. At this moment, I'm grateful the medicine is working because I don't have to search behind every door to see where she is. I could hear her snoring from the cave I woke up in a few hours ago.

I followed the sound of slobber-coated grumbles toward what I would assume was the main bedroom. I pushed open the cracked bedroom door with the index finger of my right hand, keeping the knife gripped in my left. Tiptoeing over to the bed, following the sound of her snoring, when she stops, I stop.

I stood over Melissa, watching the slobber make its way down to her neck. Sure would hate to ruin this sleep, but she has something I desperately want. I would stop at nothing to get it. My heart flutters and picks up pace while I watch her carotid artery beat against her skin like a drum. As much as I want to cut it in half, I can't. She would die too quickly, and I would miss the window to take over.

Her breathing slows, the snoring stops, and Melissa shifts in bed. Her body is tense. She can feel me, my presence. Well darn, this was enjoyable, but I don't want to listen to her obnoxious scream. I would prefer her not to wake up and see me standing over her in all black with a knife glistening in the moonlight. This stupid look on my face wouldn't make it any better.

I raised the knife to her neck and, in one swift motion, I carved a fine line from one side to the other. She woke instantly, hands flying to her neck to stop the blood. There was no point.

"Give it up, Melissa, you're going to die." I said, while licking the blood off the blade's tip.

Chapter 3: Demon

I watched as life left Melissa's eyes. I listened to her choke and gargle on her blood. Although I loved the sound, my window was approaching fast. The small window to body hop is crucial. A soul cannot leave the body for too long, or another soul can't enter. The best time to make the switch is immediately after the twinkle in their eyes is gone. When the pupils no longer react to light. The limbs grow weak and fling around like spaghetti noodles. That is the peak.

I pulled out the pre-filled syringe I had in my pocket and placed the knife in position for the encore. Her hands flopped down to her waist sides and as soon as they did, I slit the old guy's throat, my throat. Simultaneously, injecting epinephrine into Melissa's thigh.

Everything became dark and quiet. My immediate surroundings were awkwardly still. Time stopped for just a moment. I was in a free-fall descending into a bottomless, dark pit. Until I wasn't. I jumped up in a panic, taking in a large gulp of air like it was a pitcher filled with ice-cold water. I drank it down and looked around. The old guy's body wrinkled up on the floor, looking pathetic. What a total waste of space.

I focused my attention on my hands, turning them over to make sure the switch worked. Running my fingers through my hair first, then my breast, then my vagina. Yup, I am definitely a 34-year-old woman.

I climbed out of bed, onto the floor, and scrambled over to my Polaroid to snap a quick picture. I love a good souvenir. Grabbing the old guy by his ankles, I dragged him from the primary bedroom to the backyard. I had every intention of burning the old guy's body only because I didn't like to leave dead bodies lying around. Whether or not they can be identified is irrelevant to me. They cannot identify me. No matter where they look or how hard, I'm dead, non-existent.

Dragging the old guy was a piece of cake. I could say, that is a good thing that came from living as him for a while. I've gotten familiar with carrying around his bodyweight. Searching the grounds, I realized the old home provided many places to take the body to decay. *Change of plans.* Instead of wasting my time watching the old guy's body burn, I decided the crawl space under this dilapidated home would provide the house with a little extra spunk. He would make the perfect fit.

I grabbed the body by the ankles again and proceeded to the opening of the crawlspace. While breaching the entrance, mice scampered out. Thrashing through cobwebs, I crab-walked in reverse, dragging him deeper into the dark. The rats will thank me for this when they return.

I exited the crawlspace, the wind thrashing against my skin. The adrenalin finally settled, allowing me to feel sharpness from the cold air and exhaustion crashing down on me. I crossed my arms around my breasts, realizing I forgot to put on clothes.

I waltzed back into Melissa's home, intending to get dressed. My new body had other plans as the fatigue consumed me. I returned to bed, where the sheets still were damp from the pools of vital fluid. The smell of iron filled my nostrils. I ran my fingertips across the laceration on my neck. The blood clotting my incision off, closing the wound. Although bleeding to death won't kill me, choking on the stale air inside of this home might just do the trick. My eyelids kissed and in no time, I was sound asleep. That is until a loud banging from the front door caught my attention.

Goosebumps erupted in small pinpoint bumps all over me as I sat up in bed. *What the fuck?* I'm completely disoriented. The sun's rays seeping through the slits of the boards, making it obvious a few hours have passed. I'm just not sure how much time. "What day is it?" I asked myself. Thankfully, I didn't answer. I'm not that far gone. Having a conversation with myself is where I draw the line on my level of crazy.

The banging continued.

Still nude, I lazily worked my way to the front door. "I'm coming. Please stop knocking," I pleaded with the palm of my hand planted over my forehead. I have an excruciating headache.

"Ms. Gardner, this is Claireville City Police. Open the door," I heard an officer say.

My eyelids flung open, realization from the other night hitting me at once. *Shit.* I scrambled to Melissa's room and got dressed. Not forgetting to fling a scarf around my neck to cover the scar. I slipped the pocketknife into my pocket and resumed my quest to the front door.

Slinging the door halfway open, I left my torso exposed while hiding the bottom half of my body behind the door. The blade resting in my right hand, ready to get stabby just in case one of these officers tries me.

"Good morning, officers. How may I help you?" I asked with

a smile on my face and a southern accent coating my voice.

Chapter 4: Demon

The officers paid me a visit to perform a wellness check. Apparently, I have a job I have not shown up for in three days. They were kind enough to tell me where I worked and the name of my boss, who was the one to call it in. I guess showing up for work and making a little extra money won't kill me.

I wasn't able to find a towel or a rag, but Melissa's body reeked. Skipping a shower was not an option today. However, the smell isn't as awful as the body beginning to decay under the house. That's a plus.

At least she had all-in-one body soap. Men usually bathe with body soap that promises to clean everything acting as an anti-bacterial and shampoo. Women usually have twenty products to clean with. Not Melissa.

I set the shower to boil and stepped in. Steam quickly engulfed me. I lathered the soap in my hands and rubbed it into my skin. Mentally trying to sift through the files in my head that would take me back to sex education class in grade school. Staring at my new vagina, I can't figure out how to wash this thing. Soap or no soap? Do I put soap in the hole or not? It is self-cleaning right?

I thrashed a few suds through the slits and in the hole. You only live once. Worst-case scenario, I may get a yeast infection if I cleaned it wrong. Doesn't matter, I don't intend to stay in this body that long.

I dripped dry while finding something to wear. Long sleeves, a hoodie, and my handy scarf. This scarf will be my best friend for a while because it will take some time for the neck laceration to heal. It will probably still scar, however, right now it's beefy red and I don't want to draw attention to it.

I fiddled with the keys to Melissa's Pontiac, mapping out my plans for the day. Slipping out the front door and into the car, I fired up the engine. Just like Melissa when I slit her throat, the car spat and sputtered before leveling out. I drove off down the dirt road, making my way to town.

I stopped at a local Fish and Chips along the shore. The countryside doesn't allow me the luxury of breathing in the salty breeze, allowing the microscopic particles to pierce the inside of my nares. I've visited this establishment many times, as many people, but never as Melissa.

The vibe is normally upbeat. In a small town, where everyone knows one another, they usually are welcoming and greet you as soon as you enter. Not this time. The sound of clinging glass and chatter dropped dead as soon as I sauntered through the front door. Stares bore through me, causing heat to rise and spread throughout my skin. I pretended to ignore it as I walked over to the counter to place my order.

Cracked oyster shells lined the counter from previous cus-tomers. The foam still settled at the bottom of empty beer glasses left behind. Ian walked over to me from behind the counter, stuttering on his steps. His mouth fell open for a second, ready to catch a fly before asking, "Me- Melissa, how can I help you today?"

I peered over my shoulder, looking behind me at all the eyes still focused on my frame. Quietness fills the room. "Two 4 oz. salmons please," I say. Confidence in my voice as I turned around to face Ian again.

Ian is a nice kid. I'm not sure how he knows Melissa, but I know him from the many points of view of the different versions of people I met him as. He has worked here since he was old enough to remember. Running the family business by going out on his boat, catching sea creatures, and serving guests who come here day and night.

"Co-, coming right up." He sputtered.

Ian turned to face the kitchen, making his way to place my order with the kitchen staff. Meanwhile, small chatter slowly fills the room. I listened in as my order was being prepared. Not able to catch the details, I knew for certain the chatter was about me.

My order came fast, and I left that hole in the wall even faster. Racing, I headed to my storage unit while ripping through the raw salmon, smashing my foot on the gas pedal. I've been out of touch for a few days. I only needed to swipe my laptop from the unit and head back to Melissa's place. A quick grab and go.

With my laptop riding safely in the driver's seat, I drove down the dirt road leading to Melissa's house, but something was off. Blue and red lights starburst across the sky. I slow the Pontiac down from full speed to a slow creep. Clouds of dust fly past because of the sudden change in velocity.

As the dust settled, literally and figuratively, I saw a clear glimpse of the crowd surrounding the home. Dogs sniffing the grounds, officers in uniform searching. Channel 3 News didn't even want to miss this party. I knew this would come, just didn't plan for it to be this soon. I knew I should have burned the old guy. His rotten ass is still causing trouble.

I shifted the car in reverse, cruising backward down the dirt road. Obviously, I have to lie low. I'm sure Melissa is a prime suspect in this murder. I've only been in this body for a few days and the bitch is already becoming a pain in my ass.

Chapter 5: Heather

I could hear the waves crashing against the rocks outside of my window. The cool, salty breeze seeps through the small crack I left open. It is cloudy, as it always is. I lie in bed wondering what today would bring. What type of mishap or excitement would I be experiencing today?

That was when my sister burst open through my closed bedroom door and screamed, "Heather, turn on the news! There was a murder in Claireville last night."

I sat up in bed quickly, thrusting forward shot the sheets away from my chest. Scrambling for the remote, as I hate to miss juicy information, I finally felt cold plastic in my hands. Vision still blurry, I ran my fingers across the rubber buttons until I found the biggest round button at the top of the remote, showing it was for power. I gave it a light tap and the news channel immediately came on the screen, streaming last night's mayhem.

"Last night, terror struck Claireville. It has been five years since our last homicide. At approximately six thirty this morning, police discovered a body under the house sitting behind me. Authorities have classified this crime as murder, although we are still waiting for the coroner's report. There was a deep slit at the throat of a 72-year-old man which sliced his carotid artery and caused him to bleed until his gruesome death. We have not identified the victim yet, but will work tirelessly to solve this mystery. Until we do so, keep your doors locked and be aware of your surroundings. Thank you for choosing Channel 3 News. Now for your weather report."

"There will be cloudy skies with a hint of-," The sound of a male voice echoed in the background as I stopped listening once there was no more information given about the murder last night.

What is going on in Claireville? This is hitting too close to home.

Claireville is a small town, not much happens here. I leave my doors unlocked, for Christ's sake. I don't know martial arts. I never thought I needed to learn. People here are like family. We look out for each other. I couldn't think of anyone who would be capable of killing a sweet old man in cold blood.

I shook the trembling off and gathered myself, trying not to process what may or may not have happened last night, and waltzed over to the doorway of the bathroom. Not realizing I had been standing in the same spot for I'm not sure how long, staring at my feet when my sister chimed in. "Heather, are you okay?"

Slowly making my way to the vanity mirror, I gave myself a quick overview and damn; I look like shit. Mascara smeared under my eyes from the night before gives me the appearance of someone as lifeless as the man found in Claireville last night.

I trotted over to the shower, deep in thought. The warm water hitting my skin caused me to get lost in contemplation. I need more excitement in my life. After graduating from college, I continued living at home with my dad. He is in no rush to kick me out and I am in no rush to bury myself in debt with bills. However, my journalism career hasn't exactly taken off yet.

My only obligation is to care for my younger sister, Rosie. She is supposed to graduate high school next year which makes her practically independent. With our dad never home, it is usually just us. I prefer to keep myself locked in the room most of the time, digging up information and journaling, of course.

I switched the shower off and grabbed a towel, wrapping it around me. I threw my hair in a high, messy bun and prepared myself to deliver the news I just received from Channel 3 to my dedicated followers.

I'm grateful for being a part of this day and age. Where my generation refuses to depend on the news channel for information. They would prefer to get their spill from the internet. Journaling takes consistency. Updating my followers daily and promptly keeps them happy. Still, I need one break. Not secondary information already shared on another platform, but a break where I investigate a case and share the news before any detective, officer, or especially, news reporter does.

I position myself in front of my computer, toggling the mouse to get the screen to wake. I created *SpillSecrets* during my freshman year of college. In the beginning, I used it to gossip about my classmates. Just like that time when a freshman caught our English professor watching porn at his desk while we were taking a written exam. Then the gossip turned into investigative work, like when we attempted to figure out who dug up the grave of our previous dean.

SpillSecrets became a small online community. Although I have never met my followers in real life, I still have grown close to them. They depend on me and look forward to my updates.

I began typing about the information I regurgitated from the report. My followers commented on the blog as soon as I hit submit. Cory303 was the first to make his presence known.

Cory303: Heath, good morning. Glad to see you up early spilling the secrets.

Cory303 typed using my screen name.

Me: It has been five years since our last investigation. I know it went cold, but this could be redemption. Are you ready to put in the work?

Cory303: I live for this Heath. This won't be like it was five years ago. I will eat, shit, and breathe this case until it's solved.

MidnightMuse: I'm in.

MurderEgo: I'm in.

LunaLunaLuna: In!

ByteBender: You got it.

New user joined the chat

Typing...

CrypticCrawler: Did you guys investigate the death of the man who burned in a house fire?

Cory303: And who the hell are you?

Chapter 6: Demon

Who the fuck does this Cory303 guy think he is? Alright, I get it. I'm the new guy and everyone is on edge. Little do they know; I have been watching this chat for years. It was just time I joined in on the fun. Turning my attention away from the computer, I listened as it continued to ping from the incoming comments. They were pissed, but still curious about my identity.

I slipped out the Polaroid picture and stood in front of my mural. Years of my life spent in this storage unit, in this spot, in front of this board. I pinned the picture of the old guy to the corkboard. "I will never forget you, you old hag," I said as I kissed my two index fingers and placed them on the picture of Hank.

I stepped back to appreciate my work. It isn't much, but it is a start. Roman Volkov's picture sits at the top. A large 8x10 in. photo of a Russian male, age 42, with jet-black hair slicked back. In a sinister style, the tails of his lips twisted upward, harboring a half-cracked smile. He's wearing a black tailor-made suit. He is always in a suit. Always ready to conduct business deals with the shady people at the port. My mouth waters with how badly I want to cross him off the list.

A thumbtack sits at the bottom of his photo with a piece of yarn connecting Roman's picture to a photo of his daughter. Icy blue eyes stare at me. Her jet-black hair casts a striking contrast to the color of her eyes. She looks haunted. If I had a father like hers, I would also feel haunted. Everyone's nightmare is under the same roof. She's oblivious to that, though. She thinks her father's full-time job is to run the coffee shop that sits a few blocks away from Fish and Chips.

The coffee shop sells the best coffee in town, but that is a front. Something to keep the IRS off his back. Roman is the biggest organ trafficker in history. Selling and trading organs for money. Claireville creates the perfect location for trafficking. The town is small and easy to manipulate. We are close to the water, which is where Roman conducts his business. The port is where he spends most of his time. Receiving his shipments of missing people who aren't entirely aware of their doom.

With the police force in Roman's pocket, that only leaves one person capable of bringing him to his demise. To the town, Roman is the savior. He lines the pockets of citizens who are helpless. He helps to take homeless people off of the street. Picture perfect if I don't say so myself.

Killing Roman is more than taking down a bad guy. This is personal. I have dreamed about the moment I get to slit Roman's throat for years. I don't have any intentions of slitting my own and injecting Roman with epinephrine. No, that's not the plan. I plan on returning a very personal favor to him that only he would understand. I let out a moan of pleasure from daydreaming of how Roman's skin would feel penetrating beneath my blade.

I removed a knife from my pocket and flicked it open. I twirled the knife in my fingers, weaving it through my fingertips with a swift motion, stopping to take a glance at my reflection in the blade. Then I swiftly drew my arm back and with the force of a thousand suns, I hurled it at the picture of Roman. The blade stuck to the photo, landing directly in the gap between his eyes.

I pulled my attention back to the computer screen.

Cory303: Hey you freak! Did we scare you off?

Heath: All newcomers are welcome. Don't scare away our friend.

Cory303: We have had this chat for years. Newcomers never enter. I'm just saying it's sus.

LunaLunaLuna: Cory is right. We all started here originally and never had any newcomers.

CrypticCrawler: There is a first time for everything, right? You will like me. I promise.

Cory303: People break promises.

CrypticCrawler: Good thing I never break mine. *wink*

Chapter 7: Heather

I walked downstairs to the kitchen, where the smell of freshly brewed coffee did not disappoint. Passing by the pot and opening the cabinet, I pulled out a coffee mug and began pouring my coffee, fixing it to my liking. After the first sip, I spun around to face the television screen. The picture of the home from the report earlier this morning appeared again on the screen.

I scrambled to get the remote in my grasp to turn the volume up. The police have made a breakthrough with the murder of an elderly man last night. "We have identified the victim to be Hank Frayer. The deceased has been dead for a few days, according to the coroner's report. Our thoughts go out to Hank Frayer's family." The woman stated while holding her hand up to the earpiece.

Currently displaying a picture of Hank, she continued to report, "Officers from the scene informed us that while they were performing a wellness check on the tenant of the home behind me, they could smell the stench of a decaying body. We are grateful for our police force here in Claireville. We will not release the name of the suspect at this time, however, we will provide more information on this case as they arise. Again, thank you for choosing Channel 3 News."

I sipped my coffee on the couch now with my legs crossed. Mind racing a thousand miles a minute. Hank Frayer. I know of him. I just can't remember where from. Maybe it will come to me later.

The sound of the front door slamming shut snapped me out of my reminiscing. My head snapped in that direction. "We are going out tonight." Rosie quirked.

I scrunched my face. "No, we're not."

I don't like a crowd. Rosie knows that, but she hates going out alone. Usually, we compromise, and last time she stayed home for me.

"Actually, yes we are. I already brought our dresses." She said with enthusiasm and a smile that I can't say no to planted across her face.

"Ok. Ok, Rosie. Where are we going?" I asked, rolling my eyes.

"Oh, you know, the pub."

"You know what happened last time we went there, Rosie. Don't make me go back."

"That won't happen again. No worries."

I snatched the bag from her hand and stomped off. This dress better be cute if she's dragging me out of the house.

Cute is an understatement. This dress is to die for, but whose funeral is it?

In a snug, form-fitting fabric, this dress gently hugs every curve, offering a comfortable fit. As I run my fingers down the fabric, I'm struck by its intense softness, enjoying the sensation. Rosie's effort to change my mind seems to have worked, at least for now.

I took my time contouring my makeup, placing highlighter where it mattered. Caked mascara was already on my lashes, yet I still applied more. I painted red on my lips and rubbed them together, evening out the lipstick. I felt gorgeous. There weren't many moments where I could bask in my femininity, where I felt beautiful.

Rosie joined me in my room, both of us looking in the standing mirror. Making sure all bases are covered, we checked ourselves out from multiple angles.

"Hey. Did you know who Hank Frayer was?" I asked, while checking out my backside in the mirror.

"Of course, I know Hank. You know him too. You act like you don't remember." She said as she stopped to look at me.

Without awaiting my response, she grabs my arm and leads me out of the room.

"Don't worry about it right now. I don't want to ruin the night. We will talk about it later." She says as she grabs her keys from the counter and leads me out the door.

Hank Frayer.

Chapter 8: Demon

The pub was full of people tonight. I needed to get out of the storage unit and mingle with people to scope out my next victim. It's only a matter of time before they arrest me for the old guy's murder. When they take Melissa, I want her to be good and dead. I will not be going to jail in her body.

I placed my order at the bar for a gin and tonic. Normally, I take my liquor straight, savoring the burn I feel as the liquid slides down my throat. I opted not to seem so manly.

A familiar voice moused up next to me, "Why did you show your face today at Fish and Chips? You know you're not welcome there?"

I turned to face Ian, who has the balls to approach me now when he practically shat himself earlier. If only he knew who the hell he was talking to, I think he would retract that statement.

I responded in the most innocent voice Melissa's vocal cords could muster, "What do you mean, Ian?"

I'm not being funny. I don't know why Melissa isn't welcome there, but I could sense that I was about to find out as Ian's face became filled with anger.

"Melissa, please don't you fucking play with me right now." He said with agitation radiating from his skin.

"Go ahead Ian, tell me. What did I do?" This time, the question was genuine. I wanted to know without making it obvious that I was completely unaware.

"My little brother still has nightmares. He's 10 and still wets the bed. He is in therapy for Christ's sake because of you," he seethed.

"And who the hell is your little brother?" I inquired. Now getting sick of his games.

"Logan, you creep. My little brother is Logan."

"Logan?"

"Yes. Logan. Like the one you raped when you were supposed to be babysitting? That Logan." His fist balled at his side, ready to slam into me, but not in front of a bar full of people.

I stared down at the countertop. How did I miss this? I knew Melissa took advantage of Logan, true. I skipped the part of Ian being his older brother. Now, with Ian towering over me, essentially foaming at the mouth, it makes sense. Logan is his half-brother. Logan has nothing to do with Fish and Chips because they don't share the same father, only the same mother.

Glancing up at Ian, I responded, "I forgot. I'm so sorry," while returning my stare to the countertop. It was sincere.

I am sorry. Now it makes sense why I received so many blank stares. I wish I could share with Ian how Melissa's wrongdoing got her killed. What she did to Logan is why I slit her throat. Then I would have to explain who I am, and I can't do that. Nor would Ian believe me.

He threw his fist, which is now bloodless from being balled up too long, into the tabletop. Bringing his face closer to mine, his hot breath almost melts my eyelashes. "If you ever step foot in my family's establishment again, I will kill you myself."

Empty threat, but I'll take it.

He heads for the door, but Rosie stops him, planting a kiss on his cheek. She's consoling him. I downed the gin and tonic in one gulp. Rising from the stool, I yell out, "Ian?"

He faces me, looking like a rabid dog. He stomps over in my direction, ready to tear the flesh from my bones. Daring me to challenge him.

I dropped my head to the floor and spoke, "I'm ready to pay for what I've done. I don't deserve to live."

Tears well in my eyes, streaming down my cheeks.

Ian straightens, placing his shoulders back, and raising his chin. He finally responds, "Well, you better have another drink."

Head still down, I pivot to turn facing the bar again, and sneakily paint a twisted smile on my face.

Chapter 9: Heather

Me: It's been a few days and we haven't heard from Cryptic-Crawler. Do you guys not find that weird?

Typing...

Cory303: I'm glad he's gone. I don't trust him.

Me: We were all strangers at one point, too. You haven't even given them a chance.

Cory303: I would rather get to the case. What do we know about Hank?

Me: Cory, lighten up.

Cory303: Not a chance.

LunaLunaLuna: He's the town drunk. Isn't that all there is to know?

Me: Luna, there is a story here. Something more than just being at the wrong place/wrong time.

ByteBender: Heath. Do you have any updates on the case?

Me: Hank was indeed a drunk. He lived on the streets mostly, begging for money. Until a few years ago. He hasn't panhandled. He hasn't slept under the bridge, as far as anyone knows.

Cory303: A few years ago? How long exactly? These things need specifics.

LunaLunaLuna: I think 4, maybe 5 years.

Cory303: That's fishy.

MurderEgo: There's been an update on the case.

MidnightMuse: They just named a primary suspect.

Cory303: Spit it out already. Who is it?

Typing...

Me: Melissa Gardner

MurderEgo: What?

LunaLunaLuna: Okay. I'm surprised, but I'm not surprised. She's a weirdo. Totally capable.

Cory303: Why would Melissa kill Hank?

Me: Good question.

Chapter 10: Demon

My head is throbbing, and my neck is on fire. Too much to drink would have been my first assumption, but that doesn't relate to the stiffness in my neck. A strong blow attacks me from behind. Knocking the air out of my lungs and tipping me over.

I hit the ground with force, the right side of my head ping-pong off the floor. It's freezing. I'm strapped to a chair with my arms tied behind my back.

"You're finally awake, you whore?" Ian spits.

Taking a peek around, I notice fresh carcasses. Already scaled, meat taken, bones discarded. It smells like fish, so I can only assume those are fish bones and I'm in the freezer at Fish and Chips. Smart play. He could butcher me alongside the rest of the meat in here. The mixture of blood would make it hard to identify Melissa. I have to hand it to Ian, even I wouldn't have thought of this.

"Speak up! I want to hear what you have to say." He continued.

He's trying to have a conversation, hear me confess. That's not why I'm here.

"Melissa, stop acting as if you've never been drugged before. Your neck isn't what you should be worried about."

"What should I worry about then, Ian?" I challenge.

He circles me and squats to my level. "You should be in fear for your life."

"That, I'm not, but good try."

His steel-toe boot meets my face. Smashing my nose hard enough, I could hear the crack. Pain sears through my body as the blood oozes out of my nose and down my cheek. I'm so screwed up, I attempt to lick at the stream of crimson. My tongue danced around my cheek as I inch my head back, hoping by doing so, it would make my tongue long enough to reach.

"You're more fucked up than I thought." The disdain is clear. "Why did you do it?" He asks, removing a knife, which I'm guessing he uses for descaling.

"I will tell you, but you need to cut me loose. I'm not here to be tortured. Make this fair. Man vs man. Well, woman vs man. You already have the upper hand."

"Why did you do it?" He asks again.

My patience and self-control have left the building. "Because he wanted me to," I screamed.

It was a lie. I don't know why Melissa did it and it's too late to ask her.

Before I had time to process what I'd said, Ian sunk the knife deep into the side of my leg. His chest heaving, rising and falling with force. I scramble to get my hands free to nurse my leg, but my hands won't break the bondage.

"Take the knife out. Please take the knife out, Ian," I pleaded.

He shakes his head as he turns away and heads for another knife.

"Oh, no, sweetie. I don't want you to bleed to death. I have more in store for you."

I underestimated Ian. To me, he was a child, following in

his dad's footsteps. The only thing I thought he could carve, is a fish. Here I am, bound to a chair in the freezer where he plans to butcher me. At any other time, I would have found it impressive. Maybe even tried to recruit him.

He tilts his head down, eyes darkening as he approaches me. I can see twinkles in his eyes. Whatever he has planned next, he's excited about it. I don't plan on finding out. He grabs the chair and pushes it over until I'm in an upright position.

The blood from my nose pooled into my mouth. I drank it like it was a part of the last supper. Gravity benefiting me, and if it was tangible, I would kiss gravity right now.

My breath hitches and my heart rate picks up speed. Adrenalin surges through my body, but I work hard to hide it. Containing my excitement.

"Ian," I pleaded, "my nose is broken and I'm certain I can't put any weight on this leg. Please untie me. Make this fair. Do this right."

I hear the blade soar through the air and splice one bondage-free. Breaking away my right hand.

"You're not getting untied. I'll give you one hand to tend to your pathetic ass wounds."

That's all I need.

Putting pressure on my leg, I wrap my hand at the base of the knife, doing what little I can. Ian's watching as I'm sobbing and agonizing over the pain. Squirming under his gaze, he approaches me with an electric knife. Hitting the power button, he held it like an air saw, sawing the air like a madman. I cringe. This is like using a bazooka to kill a mosquito.

He bends at the waist and whispers, "You're going to feel what Logan felt, only worse. This knife is going to slice through your chest just to give me a start. Then, I'm going to dig my finger under the flap and pull your skin off, tugging and ripping it." He licks his lips and comes closer.

He continues with a whisper in my ear, "When you die from the extent of your injuries, I plan to take you far out on the boat and throw you overboard. Letting the fish finish you. How does that sound?"

"Sounds like you're full of shit," I say before taking my hand, grabbing the knife from my leg and slicing his throat.

He falls to the ground, shaking and clawing at his neck. They all react the same. I act quickly, undoing the bondage to free my other hand. Trying to ignore the intense pain I feel in my leg.

Ian's body goes limp and I'm still scrambling to find my syringe. The light in his eyes has gone and I fear I may miss my chance. I pop the cap on the syringe, stab the epinephrine in Ian's thigh and slit my throat.

Chapter 11: Demon

I had a hard time deciding what to do with Melissa's body. Ian's idea of letting the fish pick her off was superb. Hard to top that. But I want Claireville to have closure. I want Logan to see his predator and know that she can never come back to haunt him. So I decided against throwing Melissa overboard.

Instead, I cleaned up the mess of blood and anything left behind that would tie Ian to Melissa's murder. Now here we are, Melissa's corpse in the back seat, strapped in a seatbelt on the way back to that shabby house Hank died under.

Every time I look in the rearview mirror and see Melissa's head bobbing up and down from the lack of control, I get nauseous. I tried to keep my focus straight ahead.

I thought it would be iconic to put her back in bed where I found her and killed her for the first time. So I recreated the scene, without the snoring part, of course. I was even being nice by covering her up before taking out my Polaroid to snap a picture.

I stayed longer than expected because I needed to shower. The storage unit doesn't offer me that luxury. Blood from both Melissa and Ian circled the drain as the hot water beat on my skin. I doused shampoo in my hair, scratching deep into my scalp as well. I soaked Melissa's toothbrush in bleach and scrubbed my nails with it. Getting rid of every piece of her I can. Being in her body made my soul feel infected.

I threw on some of Melissa's clothes and stole a scarf, intending to burn these later. Snatching my Polaroid and picture, I left as quickly as I could, headed toward my unit. Never to return.

I screwed in the light bulb to illuminate the space in the unit. Changing out of Melissa's crap, I opted to wear what I've grown used to, Hank's clothes. Once comfortable, I pulled out the Polaroid picture of Melissa. Placing it on the corkboard next to Hank's.

"I did you both a favor. Now you two can be together again. To burn in hell, forever." I kissed my two fingers and placed them on the picture of Melissa.

Grabbing a beer from the mini fridge and my laptop from the table, I plopped down onto my mattress with both in hand. Cracking open the beer, I took a sip while also turning on my laptop. Needing to catch up on what I've missed.

CrypticCrawler: Did you guys miss me?

LunaLunaLuna: Oh buddy.

Cory303: Not in the least. Why did you return? Go back into hiding. Things were better that way.

CrypticCrawler: I wasn't hiding.

Heath: Then, where were you?

Typing...

CrypticCrawler: Business trip

Cory303: Cut the shit Cryptic. Who are you?

CrypticCrawler: Are we on a first-name basis now?

MurderEgo: You have to give us a reason to trust you.

CrypticCrawler: In time, you will know.

LunaLunaLuna: What does that even mean?

MidnightMuse: It means he has something planned, and in time, he will show us what that is.

CrypticCrawler: Exactly what Midnight said. I'm starting to like you.

MidnightMuse: Well, I don't like you.

CrypticCrawler: No one does.

Heath: Is that right?

CrypticCrawler: You should know better than anyone, Heath?

Heath: How so?

CrypticCrawler: Because you witnessed how they treated me at the pub the other night..

Heath: Melissa?

Cory303: No fucking way Melissa is in this chat. I'm not going for it.

Bytebender: What did I miss?

MidnightMuse: Melissa isn't stupid enough to join this chat. She knows she isn't welcome.

CrypticCrawler: Melissa isn't stupid enough to join this chat because Melissa is dead.

Heath: How do you know?

Typing...

CrypticCrawler: Just watch Channel 3 News tomorrow. Now you'll have something to talk about. Something to help with your little 'investigation'. Goodnight.

I shut the computer while it still chimed and dinged. Not caring to read the responses. Not caring they know about Melissa's death before the media does. No one cared about her anyway and they can't link me or Ian to a damn thing.

Chapter 12: Heather

I woke up at the crack of dawn, hoping Melissa's body was discovered by now. I couldn't bear to miss the news this morning. Wiping the crust from my eyes, I walked to Rosie's room.

"Rosie, wake up. Come downstairs." I said with one eye open. The other I'm still rubbing, trying to wake.

Rosie's room was empty. She's always on the move, doing something. We are total opposites. I would rather stay cooped up in my room, on my computer, and she would rather stay busy doing anything that doesn't include being home.

I made it to the kitchen, turning the television on to Channel 3 and making sure the volume was all the way up before starting breakfast. I rarely cook. It takes my time away from other things, like looking up the latest gossip. I know my interest in journaling isn't necessarily essential. If all blogs ceased to exist tomorrow, I would be dumbfounded, but I would live to see another day.

I took my coffee, along with scrambled eggs, toast, and turkey bacon, over to the couch. Sitting crisscrossed, I devoured my food when the familiar face of the reporter came across the television. In the background is the recognizable home where Hank died.

After a long, blank stare at the screen, the reporter began speaking. "We have a break in the case of Hank Frayer. A few days ago, someone discovered Hank's decaying body under the home behind me. Well, as coincidental as this may seem, we found the body of our prime suspect inside the home this morning. We found Melissa Gardner, ex-wife of Hank Frayer, dead in bed."

Ex-what?

The reporter continued, "Melissa died in the same fashion as Hank. Melissa was a prime suspect in the murder of Hank. However, because of additional evidence, it was determined that Melissa was a victim herself. We ask that you continue to be safe as the police force is still on the hunt for a killer on the loose in Claireville. As always, thanks for choosing Channel 3 News."

The fork I was using to stab my eggs with still hanging from my mouth. I stared at the screen long after the weather report wrapped up. Ex-wife? I know I need to update the blog, but I need a second to process this.

To the best of my knowledge, someone discovered Hank decaying under Melissa's house. The police did a wellness check on Melissa and smelled the dead body. So she must have smelled the dead body also? I'm not sure. From the look of that house, there were probably a lot of aromas swimming around in there.

Focus Heather. The officers found Hank and determined Melissa was a suspect. Melissa and Hank were married. *I need to find out when they got divorced.* Melissa goes to the pub, has a few drinks, then ends up dead in her bed from a slit throat. Hank and Melissa dying the same way.

I run up to my room, forcing my computer awake, and

heading to *SpillSecrets*. My fingers moved a mile a minute, laying out what I knew or what I thought I knew. Putting the pieces together so my online minions can pull them back apart.

LunaLunaLuna: Maybe that is why Hank was a homeless drunk. He was mourning a marriage that didn't work out.

Me: That may be part of the reason, but we have to dig deeper. Is anyone able to find out when Hank and Melissa divorced?

Cory303: I'm on it.

MidnightMuse: Is no one going to ask the most obvious question?

Cory303: If it's so obvious, why haven't you asked yet?

MidnightMuse: How the hell did Cryptic know Melissa was dead before the police found her?

Typing...
Blank message

Chapter 13: Demon

Relaxing in bed, I scrolled through my phone, Ian's phone. Figured I would get caught up on everything my new life offered. I especially needed to be familiar with how things ran at Fish and Chips. Running the restaurant isn't a problem, but I have never been fishing in my life. I'm going to have to make up every excuse not to get on the boat.

I searched through the calendar for my days scheduled to work at Fish and Chips. I searched through pictures of Ian and Rosie, anniversary dates, holiday pictures, and trips. They were a happy couple. Scrolling through his messages, I focused on the ones from Rosie.

When I was Hank, I didn't have to worry about this. They had already divorced years before I came along. I didn't need to keep up with a relationship. This thing between Rosie and Ian, its unfamiliar territory for me. Not sure how to navigate it. I can't screw it up. Ian is a stepping stone to get closer to Roman.

The port, where Roman conducts his business, is visible from the docks at Fish and Chips. Working there will give me a little extra cash, but that's not what I care about most. I care about the intel.

Ian's phone dings and a message banner pops up at the top

of the screen. Pulling my attention away for a moment. A message from Christophe:

"Bring the crowbar tonight. I will send over the serial numbers of the containers I need you to pop open. Don't be late."

My finger traces the screen. Just the excitement I needed. First hand in on the action. I want nothing to do with this shit. I just have to play by the rules to get closer to Roman. Once he dies, that will put a major halt to the trafficking in Claireville.

After you cut off the head of a snake, a new one will grow in its place. I will not stop trafficking. It's just not possible and I am aware of that. As long as I can be present when Roman takes his last breath, I don't care what happens after.

I respond. "I'll be there."

That's something Ian would say. Trying to sound all cool and shit.

I send a message to Rosie since I'm on a roll. "I'll be busy tonight. Fish and Chips business."

The three bubbles form at the bottom of the screen while Rosie was responding. After a long wait, I give up. I set the phone down and picked up my computer, heading to *SpillSecrets.*

CrypticCrawler: Aw, man. I missed all the action this morning. You guys couldn't wait for me?

Cory303: You must have been tired from all the murders you've been committing.

Heath: Cory!

Cory303: What Heath, it's true. You know it's him.

Heath: We don't even know if it is him or her. You never asked.

Cory303: It doesn't matter. You know it's a strong possibility he, she, or whatever, is who killed Melissa and Hank.

CrypticCrawler: Hey now Cory. You're hurting my feelings.

Cory303: How did you discover Melissa was dead before the police found her? You can't lie. There's only one answer to that question that makes sense.

CrypticCrawler: If there is only one answer to the question that makes sense, then why are you asking?

Ian's phone chimes. A message from Rosie.

"Where were you last night?"

Shit.

Chapter 14: Heather

Cory303 has a very valid point. The problem is, I love good gossip. Maybe a little murder story here and there, but I don't want to be this close to the murder. If CrypticCrawler killed Melissa and Hank, that's his business. I mean, Melissa probably deserved it. Hank, however, I'm uncertain. I still can't remember whether I'm supposed to know who he is.

My room door swings open and my attention shoots over to what, or who, is standing in my doorway.

"I was thinking you forgot where you live," I said as I eyeballed the dad I hadn't seen in over a week.

"I brought you something," He spoke. Sure he did. He always brings us things when the guilt eats at his conscience.

He crept over toward my bed as if he was afraid I would bite. Never know. I just might. A black box in his hand wrapped in a sparkly gold bow. He extended his arm to my reach, and I grabbed the box.

Unraveling the bow slowly, to not seem too ecstatic, I opened the box to reveal its content. A small, black remote with four buttons on it. I flipped it over to see the Range Rover emblem embossed on the back. I looked up at him and smiled.

"You bought me a car!" I exclaimed.

He stared at me, opting not to respond. Instead, he just

smiled.

"The coffee shop is doing well, I see. Business must have picked up." I comment while still admiring the remote.

I jumped off the bed, realizing the actual car awaited me outside. Gathering my house shoes and darting out the door, laptop in hand, I stood at the entrance of the garage and there she was. A beautiful all-white Range Rover with shiny chrome rims to complement. The interior is red with fine, even stitches that scream luxury.

I jumped in to hear the engine purr. The start was smooth, the engine quiet. Before I could give him a quick hug and a thank you, his phone rang.

"This is Roman. Go ahead." He spoke. Irritation in his voice.

His voice trailed off as he walked away. Turning my attention away from his conversation, I trailed my fingers down the side of my new truck. I could hear his footsteps approach me.

"I have to go. Something just came up." Irritation turned into frustration and fury.

"Already? You just got here. I wanted to take you for a spin in my new truck." I said with disappointment.

"Maybe next time, sweetheart. This shouldn't take long." He placed the phone back to his ear and let out a loud groan. If business at the coffee shop pissed me off that badly, I would sell it.

I climbed back into the truck and decided I would take a drive alone. Taking my time, I cruised around the countryside and into town for a while before deciding to take the interstate. I wanted to increase my speed to see what she could really do. I hit Interstate 10 and applied more pressure on the gas pedal. Weaving in and out of traffic to test the handling. She drove like a beauty.

I don't leave the house often, therefore, when I do, I take in everything. All of my surroundings, including the people I pass, the pleasant homes I see, and the car that's been following me for the past 12 miles.

At first, I thought nothing of it. Figured maybe we were just going in the same direction. However, when I turned onto the interstate, they turned onto the interstate. When I got off on a random exit to fake them, so did they. I immediately got back on the interstate, they followed suit.

I weaved through traffic; they weaved too. I hit 80 mph and took a sharp exit on the nearest off-ramp, crossing over two lanes to do so. No longer seeing them in my rearview, I drove to the nearest Starbucks. Sure, I could have gone to my dad's establishment, but he doesn't have free Wi-Fi.

I exited my truck, grabbed my laptop on my way out, and locked the doors as I walked up to the coffee shop. In the windows of the shop, I saw the same car following me pass by. I peeked over my shoulder and the car parked a few spaces down from mine.

Trying not to panic, I found a seat to melt in and ordered my normal cold brew on the app. I drew out my computer and connected to their Wi-Fi. My blog awaits me. The bell rings as the door opens and my eyes shoot up, once again, to what or who was standing in the doorway.

Whoever he or she is, is making their way over to my table, looking dead at me. They grabbed a seat directly across from me and sat down.

Their eyes never leave mine.

Chapter 15: Demon

"Come over to Fish and Chips tomorrow, will you?" I sent a text to Rosie, hoping by then I could come up with a lie to tell her.

I stuffed the crowbar, oil, a pre-filled syringe, a headlamp, and a change of clothes in a black bag to take with me. I'm uncertain if I'll need all of it, but there's no harm in having it, just in case.

I've been staying at Ian's place for the past few days. Needing to get acquainted with my new life and the best way of doing so is submerging myself in everything, Ian. If you didn't know him, you would think he was on the straight and narrow. A good kid who took after his father and worked hard running the restaurant. That's only true for half of the double life he's living.

Ian's little bachelor pad is a penthouse with a studio floor plan. Windows where you can see the city surrounded the entire area. Tailor-made suits and Tom Ford custom loafers lined half of his closet. The other side contains wet shoes, knee-high water boots, smocks, and hand-me-down clothes he wears to work at the Fish and Chips.

Granted, I knew who Ian was before I killed him. Ian doing petty jobs for Roman's men is why I killed him. Therefore, none of this surprises me. Anyone who believes Ian could afford all of this on Fish and Chip's salary is a fool.

I put on one of Ian's tailor-made suits and slipped my feet into his Tom Fords. I've never gotten to wear anything this expensive. Of course, I had every intention of taking advantage of such luxuries.

Snapping the black bag over my shoulder and placing my phone in my pocket, I exited the penthouse and stepped onto the elevator. Once the doors opened on the bottom floor, I could see Christophe next to the black Tahoe waiting for me to get in.

He's dressed in his suit as well, like this is some sort of business meeting. When really, we were headed to break into a few containers containing a crap load of missing people. My stomach churns in disgust.

"Christophe." I spoke, nodding my head in his direction.

"Ian." He responded. Nodding back.

Neither of us spoke on the ride to the port. Christophe doesn't seem like he's a man of many words. I didn't care to get anything out of him. We pulled into the port, stopping at the security booth.

"Men, may I see some ID?" asked the top flight security officer.

"Roman's men." Christophe retorted.

The security guard waved us through and the Tahoe quickened, heading toward the containers. Christophe passed a sheet of paper over to me that housed the written serial numbers of each container I would have to pop open. I nodded my head to him in understanding while grabbing my bag from the seat. As soon as the Tahoe came to a stop, I jumped out.

"Meeting back here in ten?" I asked.

Christophe nodded in agreement.

I sprinted behind the first group of containers, beads of sweat appearing at my hairline. Crouching down to access the contents of my bag, I pulled out the crowbar and removed the headlamp. Placing the headlamp on my head, I read off the first set of serial numbers. A142.

I looked around for the matching container, afraid to come so close to the victims. Feels like a maze in this place. Seems like I've walked past the same containers multiple times. I finally found the one that read A142 and positioned my crowbar over the lock. The sound of the crowbar, lock, and container clashing amplified. The noise ricocheted off of the surrounding units.

I gave the crowbar a tight squeeze, and the lock popped under pressure. After removing it, I went still, so did everything around me. The noise settled and silence took over. Until the sound of whimpers reached my ears. Muffled sounds from inside the container seeped through the cracks.

There was an angel on one shoulder telling me not to open the door and a devil on the other encouraging me to go for it. My curiosity agreed with the devil, so I picked up the lever, twisted it outward, and swung open the door.

My headlamp illuminated the women and children being held captive. All races and all ages looked up at me with eyes full of fear. Some had tears streaming down their cheeks, while others had pain clear in their eyes.

The hairs on the back of my neck stood and I could hear someone behind me closing in.

"Son, are you trying to get killed?" A familiar voice said from behind me.

"Dad?"

Chapter 16: Heather

"Heath?"

I held the cold brew to my lips and stared at the person sitting across from me. I was uncomfortable and highly confused, especially since this person referred to me as my online chat name. Granted, it is very close to my actual name, which I did for a reason, but no one calls me that outside of *SpillSecrets*. Since I have met none of my online friends in person and have never heard their voices, it's hard for me to determine who is sitting in front of me right now.

"If you're CrypticCrawler and you have come here to kill me, I would suggest that you are successful on your first attempt because you won't get a second," I said with confidence. Knowing damn well I'm not capable of doing anything other than getting up screaming as I run out of here.

He laughed, "No. I'm not CrypticCrawler."

"Then who are you?" I asked, hitting my cold brew on the table with force. The liquid jumped out of the cup and on to my hand.

"Cory303." He said with a smile forming across his face.

"Any other time I would be excited to see you, but seeing as though you were following me, following a car I was just gifted not even an hour ago, creeps me out."

"I understand. I have a lot to explain."

"Then start." I retorted.

"Since you started *SpillSecrets*, I have been following your blog and dedicating myself daily to your updates."

"And?"

"And we sort of became family. So much so that I figured I needed to protect you, how families protect each other."

"Protect me from what?" I ask as my index fingers rotate around each other, implying for him to get to the point.

"From CrypticCrawler."

"That doesn't answer the question of how you found me and why do you think I need to be protected from CrypticCrawler? How long have you been following me?"

"I started tracking your computer a few years ago. I know where you live. You never leave the house. I haven't had to stalk you per se since I've always known where you were, home." He explained, while looking down at his fingertips.

He resumed, "I want to protect you from CrypticCrawler because he's dangerous."

"And how do you know that?"

"I don't know for sure. I just have a feeling."

I'm honored Cory thought enough of me to want to protect me, but I'm also uncomfortable because if he could track me, that means other people can as well. Journaling is something I wanted badly; I didn't think about the negative things that come with it. Like people forming a connection with me online, a strong connection prompting them to hack my IP address and follow me around town to protect me.

I could see him studying me while I shifted in my seat. I'm uneasy. Sure, I knew Cory, but I don't truly know Cory. I know his online presence, that's it.

He finally spoke. "Don't worry. I hid your IP address and replaced it with a fake one that shows your location is in Japan." A slight grin appeared on his face, hoping the comment would make peace with me.

I stopped shifting and looked up at him, "What are we going to do about CrypticCrawler?"

"We have to find out who he is," Cory said while leaning over to me in a whisper.

"Or she." I giggled.

"Real funny, but no way Cryptic is a she. Hank's throat wasn't slit under the house in the crawlspace because someone would have found a pool of blood underneath him. Someone murdered him and then moved his body into the crawlspace. That took strength. Not saying a woman couldn't have done that, just saying it was highly unlikely."

He has a point, but I'm still not excluding the possibility of Cryptic being a woman.

Cory began leaning over to pull something out of his back pocket. "There's something I want to show you."

He began unfolding a piece of paper and handing it over to me. Explaining the picture of a little girl, maybe 11 years old, staring up at me.

"Who is this?" I ask, while running my finger across the photo.

"Her name is Elizabeth Turner. She would be 16 now. Her father died in a house fire 5 years ago." He peered over his glasses, cocking his head down to look down at me. "The fire."

I gasped. "The fire as in the fire we investigated that went cold? That was her father who died?"

"Yes." Cory spoke.

"But no one mentioned her in the report or in the news. I

didn't find her name in anything related."

"Exactly." Cory said. "And I believe she is helping Cryptic-Crawler."

I folded my arms and responded, "But you said a woman couldn't be CrypticCrawler."

"I never said she couldn't have help."

Chapter 17: Demon

Everything was a blur as I followed my dad's hazy figure back to Fish and Chips. He finished breaking open the rest of the containers while I stood in one spot, staring down at my feet. Then he informed Christophe of the containers being ready for unloading. Here we are, headed to the restaurant. Together, weirdly.

I couldn't speak. Normally, I would have something smart or witty to say, but I couldn't say anything. I watched as he changed out of his clothes into something comfortable, more fitting.

"Get out of that suit, kid." He said to me.

I moved without thinking. Barely paying attention to what I was doing.

"What were you doing at the port?" I asked him.

Larry has always been a stand-up guy. His dad ran this business. His dad's dad ran it before and so on. They were the type of men you look up to. At least, I'm sure Ian did.

He says, "I knew one day you would find out, but I didn't think it would be like this. Our family has always worked for Roman. Generations before me have been in business with the Russians. Your great-grandpa, grandpa, me, and now, you."

I stood still, standing in my boxers, looking at Larry in

disbelief. I've done my homework. Before beginning this journey, I have thought of everything. Some things you just don't see coming, no matter how hard you look.

Larry continued, "How else do you think we keep the doors open in this place? You think selling fish and a little beer keeps the lights on, keeps the bills paid?"

He took out a cigarette, lit it, and took a long draw.

"Even if it did, you don't get out of business with Roman. There is no out." He finished. Looking at me like he wants me to be relieved that I finally know we have soul ties with a trafficking lord. I give him no response.

"There are certain things you can't do when on a job. One of those things is looking at the merchandise. That shit you pulled out on the port could have gotten you killed. A slug to the jug, you hear me?" He asked while pointing a fake gun made of his two fingers to his skull.

I finally spoke. "I understand." After a long pause, I resumed, "I just can't handle seeing or even knowing there are people against their will in those containers."

"Well, don't think about it, son. Remember, it is you or them." He said while taking another long drag and exhaling a cloud of smoke.

He's right. It's them or me. Or Roman. The heat in my veins intensified. Knowing is one thing, and seeing is another. I don't want to rush my plan on how I'm going to take down Roman, but I wish that day could be tomorrow.

I need this to go perfectly. I need to see his face when I am seconds away from killing him. Larry is staring at me like he can sense what I'm thinking.

"I know what you're thinking, son, and I had those same thoughts, too." He came over to me, getting close to my face, our noses almost touching. Baring his teeth, he said, "You better not fucking think about doing anything to Roman unless you want to get us all killed."

He took another puff, tossing the cigarette on the floor and stomping it out before walking out.

It's more than just a thought. My plan to kill Roman is already in motion. *Eat shit, Larry.*

Chapter 18: Heather

Cory and I have been meeting at the coffee shop for a few days to discuss how we would draw CrypticCrawler out of hiding. It was the only way to figure out who he was. I continued to communicate through the blog so Cryptic wouldn't be on our trail. It worked out well since the others didn't know what Cory and I were up to.

MidnightMuse: Any other updates on who killed Melissa and Hank?

Cory303: Not yet, but I'm working on it.

He typed while sitting across from me at Starbucks. We sat in the same spot almost every day. Cory showed up promptly with his laptop in tow. I've grown to enjoy our time together. Never thought I would get out of the house as often as I do to be meeting with a *friend*. The word friend sounds so weird to say.

"We have something," I think aloud. "We should tell them we know about Elizabeth."

Cory quizzed, "Wouldn't it intrigue them and coerce Cryptic to come out of hiding?"

"If not completely, at least our knowledge would alarm him." I placed the cold brew to my lips and took a few sips as Cory began typing, making notes of what we know so far.

ByteBender: No kills recently. Do you think maybe Cryptic has gone into hiding?

CrypticCrawler: Who said it was me?

LunaLunaLuna: Any updates on the case?

MurderEgo: We all know it was you.

CyrpticCrawler: Well, prove it.

Typing...

Cory's little fingers were moving as we paused and looked at each other. Knowing the comment he's about to make is going to send the chat into a tailspin.

Cory303: We don't have to work too hard to find out where you are, Elizabeth, or who's helping you.

LunaLunaLuna: Who is Elizabeth?

MurderEgo: Woah, what's going on? Cory303, something we should know about?

Me: Elizabeth is the daughter of the man who died in the fire all those years ago.

ByteBender: The fire we attempted to investigate? No one said anything about a daughter. How did you find this out?

Cory303: It wasn't easy. Somehow, they kept that information from being released. They hid it well, but I managed to find it.

MurderEgo: Why would someone need to hide the fact that a child was in the fire?

LunaLunaLuna: How is that relevant to the killings?

Cory303: I couldn't find an autopsy report, which implies that she may still be alive.

Me: It's relevant because she could have come back for vengeance.

ByteBender: Avenging her father?

Cory303: Exactly.

LunaLunaLuna: Guys, this is getting too deep.

A familiar voice was ordering coffee, and I turn my attention over to the cash register. I can tell that voice and stature from a mile away. I call to him, to join us. A familiar face would be nice to have around right now.

"Ian," I say aloud to get his attention.

He turns to look at me with a blank stare.

I continue, "Come join us." I wave my hand back and forth with my palm facing me.

He grabs his coffee and walks steadily toward us. Pulling his jacket together like people do when they're cold and uncomfortable. Or when they're hiding something.

Ian approached the table. "Ian, this is Cory." I held my hand out, signaling who I was referring to.

Looking at Cory, I added, "Cory, this is Ian. My sister, Rosie's boyfriend."

They shook each other's hand while Ian grabbed at the scarf around his neck, pulling it down so it wouldn't be as tight as a noose. A nasty scar with purplish bruising around it is visible. Cory and I snapped a look at each other.

"Cory, it was nice to meet you. Heather, I'll be seeing you soon." Ian spoke, then turned to walk off. Cory and I nosediving back into our computers.

LunaLunaLuna: So Melissa and Hank died from slits to their throats? Is this Cryptic's signature?

MidnightMuse: It would seem that way.

Me: Yes, the victims so far have all died the same way.

Cory303: Why doesn't he try something different next time? If he's so obsessed with throat-slicing, why doesn't he just hang his victims instead?

ByteBender: Cory303 that's insensitive don't you think?

Cory dropped me a dark look and I could tell what he was thinking. I let him proceed.

Cory303: It might be, but if he's a true killer, he wouldn't take the easy way out of providing a quick death. He would have to watch his victims struggle, fighting for air. I don't think he is capable of being that cruel. Which would mean he's just a copycat, doing all of this for nothing.

I look up from the computer and focus on Cory. "I think we should start linking the previous deaths to get ahead. Maybe we can figure out who is next if there is a next victim." I state.

"We have two victims already who have died at different times. I would think we are already labeling him as a serial murderer. Therefore, it's likely there will be another victim, and soon." Cory explains, never breaking from typing on his computer.

I look away to find Ian standing in one spot by the door, staring at his phone, looking ominous.

Chapter 19: Demon

Rosie met me at work to catch up on why I've been away. Ian and Rosie spent every day together. Since I've taken over for Ian, I haven't been around much and she's getting suspicious. I explained how things weren't that great lately. Without going into detail, I told her about a family secret my dad shared with me without warning. Thankfully, she was understanding.

I'll have to buy her something later. Make her forget about our minor mishap. Giving women gifts usually does the trick, or so I think.

I cashed out the register, preparing to leave for the night, when Christophe walked in. The restaurant is empty, which just leaves us. He motions for me to meet him in the office, my dad's office. I closed the register and led the way, Christophe following shortly behind.

Christophe is the first cousin to Roman, making him Roman's right-hand man. He does all the dirty work. Shows his face far more than Roman ever could. Constantly putting himself at risk, being Roman's lap boy.

He takes a seat behind the desk, in my father's chair. Webbing his fingers together, he motions for me to sit, but still no words. I follow the order.

I sit and lean back in the chair to seem relaxed. I'm the

furthest I could be from relaxing. My lips twitch and my right leg jumps up and down before placing my hand on it, begging it to stop.

Christophe begins, in a strong, Russian accent, "I heard about what happened at the port."

My lips part but no words form. Not now anyway. My mouth is dry and even if words could escape, I would probably choke on them. Literally.

"I'll give you another chance. You're young. You don't know better. Those women and children saw your face. You put yourself and me at risk." He took out a cigar and lit it, taking a long draw.

He continued, "If even one of them speaks and you fuck up this operation, you'll beg me to show you mercy." He took another long drag. Seemed like time stood still as he kept taking puffs, ashing on the desk in between draws.

He spoke. "Place your hand on the table."

I looked at him, puzzled.

Christophe leaned forward. Through gritted teeth, he repeated, "Place your hand on the table, boy."

I did as I was told. Placing my right hand on the table, spreading my fingers. Assuming we are about to play a game of Russian roulette. Christophe took another drag and quickly tore the cigar away from his mouth, positioning the cherry red tip at the center of the back of my hand.

My arm twitched from the pain, but I didn't let out a peep. I shut my eyes, squeezing them together as tightly as I could. Show no pain, ask for no mercy. He's lucky I don't slit his throat right now. Christophe wasn't on my list, but now he certainly was.

"Welcome to hell, Christophe," I say under my breath.

He put more pressure on the cigar, still with the cherry tip held against my skin.

He asked, "What did you say, boy?"

I snapped my eyes open and looked at Christophe, heart racing. *Now isn't the time. His time will come.* I answer, "Nothing. I understand. It won't happen again."

He stands, throwing the cigar in my lap, and tilting his head in agreement. Then walks out the door. I remove my hand from the table, checking the damage. Standing, I walk out and leave Fish and Chips, headed to my unit to add Christophe's picture to the corkboard.

Chapter 20: Demon

I've been hiding in my unit for a few days. Taking a step back to map out my plan. Things are changing rapidly and I needed to adapt to those changes. I take out my phone, not Ian's but the burner phone I've had since the fire, scrolling to the one contact I have on my contact list.

Lisa. Lisa has been a great friend, helping me through this journey. She keeps me sane and steers me back on track when I spiral. I hit the dial button.

It rings a few times before she answers, "Lisa?" I say before she can speak. I could hear her kids running in the background.

"Hello, this is Lisa," Lisa answers before pulling away from the phone. "Charlie, put that down." She yells at one of her kids.

"Lisa, this is Jason." I say in a low tone.

"I know who this is. Jason, are you okay? Are things going to plan?"

I plant my face in the palm of my hand. "Give me re-assurance. I don't want to wait. I want to kill them all, and I want to do it now."

"Kids, keep busy. I'll be right back. Mommy is going to step outside." I hear her yelling back to her kids again.

The line goes quiet, which lets me know she has found

somewhere more suitable to talk.

"Jason. Listen. You've come too far to allow these people to ruin your revenge. They tried to kill you years ago. Don't you remember that?"

"Lisa, don't talk to me like I don't fucking remember the worst day of my life." I spit.

"Exactly. Don't let that all be for nothing. You need to make them pay for what they did to Elizabeth. I know if anything ever happened to my babies, I would kill anyone involved and everyone who stands in the way."

I know the mission. I remember getting away from the fire, away from the house. That night, I almost died under the bridge. Still can't believe I made it out, but I'm here. I survived for a reason. That can't be in vain. My daughter is dead and they have to pay. My entire life was gone, up in smoke. I can't settle for a half-ass job. I can't rush through this and do it wrong. You can't kill the same person twice. Lisa is right.

"I've added someone else to the list. Steering away from my original path as planned." I update Lisa.

"You know the rule, Jason. If they're bad people, you have the green light to kill them. You know what you told me, what you promised me. You don't kill the innocent." She says with sincerity in her voice.

"I know. He's far from innocent, Lisa."

"Then put him in the dirt. Come home if you need to take a step back."

"No. I need to finish this. Thank you. Get back to those kids."

"Call me if you need anything." She says before the line goes dead.

I stare at the ceiling, listening to silence before tuning into the television in the background. Roman's face flashing across the screen has my full attention. I turn the volume up to listen.

He's holding up an enlarged check with him on one side and the dean of the School for Deaf Kids on the other. 9 million dollars being donated to the school. Parents of the kids all line up to shake his hand, thanking him for his contributions. Meanwhile, Roman has containers full of women and children from all over, preventing them from ever seeing their families again.

I fire up my laptop and head to *SpillSecrets*.

CrypticCrawler: You all missed me yet?

Cory303: No.

LunaLunaLuna: No. Go away.

MidnightMuse: Give up the theatrics and mind fucks. Tell us what you want.

CrypticCrawler: You want me to be honest?

Heath: Sure.

ByteBender: Yea. Like you are capable of saying anything of truth.

CrypticCrawler: I've been honest since meeting you guys. You just haven't been asking the right questions.

Cory303: Just tell us what you want.

CrypticCrawler: I want.....

Typing...

Cory303: Ugh. This guy.

CrypticCrawler. I want Roman Volkov.

Heath: Excuse me?

CrypticCrawler: You don't understand English suddenly, Heather?

Heath has left the chat.

Chapter 21: Heather

I'm shaking, and sweaty, and haven't slept a wink since last night. CrypticCrawler and my dad? He's the most upstanding citizen Claireville offers. He just donated millions of dollars to the School for Deaf Kids. He owns a reputable coffee shop. He barely spends time at home with his daughters because he's busy giving back to this community. This asshole, who is probably just pulling my tail, thinks it's okay to belittle my dad?

A thud at my window brings me out of deep thought and back to reality. Another thud at my window caused me to jump out of bed, scrambling for my robe. I crept over, pulling back the blinds before another thud sent me hurling backward.

I stood, attempting to grab some courage out of thin air and peek around the blinds. It's Cory, throwing rocks to get my attention. I open the window.

"Let me in," Cory says and walks to the front door. He didn't ask and didn't wait for an acknowledgment. He just assumed I would do it and I will. I walked down the stairs, to the front door, and let him in. He walks past me, taking in his surroundings.

"Wow, you have a nice place here." He says in astonishment.

"It's my dad's," I say dryly.

"Is it okay to talk in here, or should we go somewhere more private?" He asks, peaking around the corner as if to see if someone is listening.

"We can go to my room, but no one is here. My sister and dad are rarely home. Just me. You should know that, though." I squint one eye toward him, pointing out my suspicion of how well he keeps tabs on me.

"I keep up with you, Heather. Not your entire family. I'm not waiting outside to see who is coming and going. Please don't insult me and lead me to your room." He snaps.

We walk to the room and I shut the door, watching Cory take everything in. He motions for my desk area, asking if it is okay to sit. Without words, I motion back, telling him it is. He pulls out a folder, along with a few photos I can't make out yet, certain that soon he will show me.

"Sit, Heather." He says.

I sit on the foot of my bed, still within arm's reach of Cory. If it weren't serious, he would have waited until our meeting at the coffee shop. Coming to my home only meant this couldn't wait. Most importantly, it meant no one should hear.

"You're not going to like this, but we may be on to something." He peers at me over his glasses and continues. "I need to know after I share with you what I know, you will continue to work on this case. This is very personal to you, so I understand if you don't want to."

"Cory, what the hell is going on?"

"I need you to tell me if you will continue or not. This is a lot to handle. These papers in my hand will change your life."

I stare at Cory to gauge how bad the papers in his hands could be. He gives me no trace of whether positive or negative. I don't know him well enough to read him. I twiddle with the ends of my hair, trying to decide.

"What is it about?" I ask to help me decide what I should do.

"It's about why CrypticCrawler wants your dad." He tilts his head in a matter-of-a-fact attitude.

What I know about my dad is what he wants me to know. I know he's a great guy. He's a hard worker. I know he has taken care of my sister and me since my mom skipped out on us when we were kids. There's a lot I can say about him, and they're all great things. Things to be proud of. Nothing in the files Cory is holding in his hands could make me think otherwise.

I held out my hand. "Hand them to me. I'm ready," I say, while attempting to snatch the files from Cory.

Cory retracts before I can get them in my grasp. "If we are going to do this, we do this my way. I searched long and hard for these. I did a lot of hacking with a lot of digging to get this. My plan is to feed you a little at a time so you don't get overwhelmed."

I scrunch my face.

He asks, "Are you ready?"

"Sure, Cory. I'm ready."

Cory pulls out a mug shot of a man with jet black hair. He slicks back his hair just like my dad does. He's sporting a jumpsuit. Looks like a younger version of my dad. It couldn't be him. He's never gone to prison.

"Who is this?" I asked, squinting to pick up extra details in the photo.

"This is an old picture of Dmitri Volkov. He's your grand-father and is serving time in Grimstone National Security Penitentiary."

Chapter 22: Heather

"My grandfather is dead, and his name wasn't Dmitri." I spit. Who does he think he is? Coming into my house. Telling me about my family, who he knows nothing about.

"Hear me out, Heather. I understand you're upset, but do you really think I would waltz up in here with bullshit information and not have my facts in order?" He hands me my father's birth certificate, not breaking our locked eyes.

"Maybe you would. I don't know you well enough to say otherwise."

I study the birth certificate for authenticity, not that I would know the difference either way. From the file, Dmitri is our grandfather. The name that I knew him by, Yuri, is his middle name.

"I have an entire file here ready to explain piece by piece why CrypticCrawler wants your dad dead. Are you willing to listen, or do you want to continue sitting up in this pretty little house, typing on your pretty little blog, spilling everyone's business while being oblivious to your own?" He questions me with sass.

Ouch, that hurts.

"Go ahead." I roll my eyes.

"Dmitri is serving life in prison after being charged in a

multitude of charges while running the 'family business.'" He does air quotes around the last part.

"He got arrested for something that happened at the coffee shop?" I ask in disbelief.

"Damnit Heather. How naïve are you?"

I frown.

He continues, "Do you think Dmitri is serving life in prison for making the best cappuccinos?"

He pulls out another piece of paper. It's a high-altitude picture, overhead. From a bird's-eye view, the photo was likely taken from a drone. A glimpse of what looks like the port lies beneath.

"What is this?" I ask. Cory pulls out another photo.

I grab at my chest, watching as he continues to reveal more photos of the same fashion. A multitude of women and children are being led away from the port, boarding a government van. Other photos show captive women and children packed inside containers. All dirty, all scared, all being held against their will.

My stomach churns while my mouth waters. I tear off my robe, needing air. I dart over to the window, open it, and shove my head outside. Breathing in the cool breeze, while panting, I can feel Cory behind me. He placed a hand on my back, attempting to relax me. It's working a bit, but not nearly as much as I need it to.

I gather myself and return to my previous position at the end of my bed. With my eyes still closed, taking deep breaths, I say, "I'm ready."

He counters, "Are you sure?"

"Yes. I need this. I need to know what happens next."

"Dmitri Volkov has been running a trafficking business since he took over the business from his father. Which means-," Cory shoots a look at me.

My eyes fail to meet his gaze. I wipe the sweat off my hands on the comforter.

"It means when Dmitri left, someone had to step in his place." I squeak.

Cory probes, "And that someone is?"

"My dad. My dad took over the family business. He's the head of our family's trafficking organization." I let out a sob. Tears streaming from my face in full force.

I ask, "So it's all a front?"

"That's the next part." Cory pulls out more sheets of paper. This time, a stack of them. All are full of credit and debit transactions. While handing them to me, he says, "These are bank statements. Money being laundered from offshore accounts, into your father's business accounts for the coffee shop."

"So the coffee shop isn't in business to make the best coffee in Claireville? It's a front to launder dirty money from trafficking?" I ask, while flipping through as many bank statements as I can muster.

"Unfortunately, yes." He answers.

"So what does this have to do with Cryptic?"

"Well, you remember when we decided Cryptic could be a man working with Elizabeth?"

"Yes. Do you think my dad took her?"

"Yes, and no. I've played with the idea, but I'm not sure." He explains, "If your dad took her, someone is avenging her for being traded. This would imply that Elizabeth isn't helping Cryptic because someone would have already sold her far away from here."

After pausing to fix his glasses, he continues, "If Elizabeth wasn't traded, then she is avenging her father's death. Either way, it still points back to Elizabeth. It just makes little sense why they would remove any records about her from the case."

I ponder on the question and then answer, "Maybe she got them removed or whoever is avenging her got them removed. So she wouldn't seem like a suspect. Her information being removed was intentional."

We both sit in silence for a while, running the information through our heads.

I ask, "What was the name of Elizabeth's dad?"

"He doesn't play a part in this case because Jason is as good as dead."

"Jason?" I ask.

"Yes. Jason Turner is Elizabeth's father. Found under the bridge where the homeless people sleep, dead. His body suffered severe burns. He was dead on arrival, per the police report." Cory explained.

"I understand. There's no way he has any connection. He's a victim." I place my chin between my index finger and thumb.

"But there is something else that may be a coincidence," Cory says, while pulling out another piece of paper.

He hands it to me and I take a quick look at it. It's the police report from 5 years ago. I remember seeing these reports when we investigated this case. It didn't mean as much back then, but it makes a little more sense now.

Cory pointed at the part in the report he wanted me to pay special attention to. He said, "Look at this piece right here. Do you see who else died that night?"

I read the report and looked up at Cory while saying, "Hank Frayer."

He nodded his head in agreement.

Chapter 23: Heather

We placed the files down for a little while, taking a break from the mayhem. My mind needed time to filter before sending it into overload. I stumbled downstairs to the kitchen, removing two wine glasses. I poured red wine in both cups halfway. I turned to walk back up to my room, almost dropping the glasses, when I saw my dad standing at the mouth at the bottom of the stairs.

"Who are those for?" he asks while I peer behind him to make sure Cory isn't in view.

"Glad you could make it home," I say, trembling. The wine in the glasses sloshes from side to side because of the tremors. His eyes follow the movement of the burgundy liquid in my hands. Then he looks at me.

"Is something wrong?" he asks, looking behind him in the direction I've been casting my eyes to.

His phone rings and I couldn't be more grateful. He holds up his index finger to me and answers. "This is Roman," he says while casting dark eyes toward me.

I've never seen my dad as anything other than a patient, easy-going guy. A man who would give you the shirt off his back. Now, I'm disgusted. Disappointed would be a better word.

He hurls insults down to his phone, but takes a break to

look at me. "We will finish this conversation later." He leaves through the front door, slamming it behind him. A frame of him, my sister, and me falling to the ground, the glass shattering to pieces.

I darted up the stairs where I found Cory standing with his back flushed to the wall, listening.

"What the hell was that about?" He asks. His eyes are as wide as mine, full of terror.

I shoved a glass of wine into his chest. As though we were thinking the same thing, we downed our glasses in a few big gulps. Cory packed all of his material back into the envelopes they came in and we filed out of the house, into the garage.

We climbed into our perspective sides of the Range Rover, while the garage door crept up. Bright headlights blinding as I positioned myself in the driver's seat, starting the engine. A door slammed and footsteps approached my side of the truck.

"What the hell is going on?" Rosie barked.

"I'm not sure. Dad seemed pretty pissed from a phone call he got." I gave her the short version and continued, "I'll be back in a few." I snapped, closing my door.

Rosie pivoted, turning around while throwing her hands up, and heading to her car. She backed out and sped down the road. Her car kicked up dust as it bolted out of our neighborhood. Cory quickly snapped his seatbelt in place, hoping my driving skills would be better.

"Your place?" I ask, while looking over at Cory.

"I don't mind, but I have a lot of brothers and sisters. Will that bother you?"

"Not at all," I say as we head over to Cory's house in complete silence.

Cory's home is nice and homey. Children's toys thrown in

every corner. Dishes in the sink from dinner they enjoyed together as a family. The living room still plays cartoons, providing background noise. As we walked down the hall, I noticed little scribbles on the wall written in marker. Probably from one of his siblings trying to practice being a mini Picasso.

I enjoy the scribbles longer than necessary because his mom interrupts my admiration and says, "Oh sweetie, I'm getting that painted over soon."

She holds her hand out to meet mine. Introducing herself, she says, "I'm Lisa."

I respond, "My name is Heather. Nice to meet you."

"Nice to meet you." She quirks while tilting her head to the side. "Does Heather have a last name?"

What do you think? I don't dare say that aloud.

I respond, "Yes. Heather Volkov." I say with a smile.

She is still in my hand. Her pupils constrict and her eyes darken. Niceness returns, the fake version anyhow, and she forces a smile.

"Nice to meet you, Heather Volkov."

"Nice to meet you also, Lisa." I let go of her hand and walked away.

Cory's room is what I would envision a trading office would look like. Computer monitors along the walls feed off of two laptops and a desktop. Each screen houses unique pictures. The main computer screen showcases a black background with white lettering flashing across. Intricate gadgets lie on the desk, one being a headset with a microphone attached. *SpillSecrets* pulled up on one monitor, the chat dinging from incoming messages, missing our presence. I switched my attention away from his nerd dungeon and focused on Cory.

"Tell me more about how Hank died," I said while sitting on

the edge of the bed.

"Yes. Let's get back to where we were. Hank died the same night as Jason. They were both found under the bridge. Only Hank was resuscitated. Jason couldn't be. They found Hank overdosed and gave him Narcan. He responded to it for a little while, but soon after, his heart stopped. He was resuscitated before being transported to the hospital."

Maybe that's where I remember Hank from—seeing him in an article after having a near-death experience.

"That is an odd coincidence. Were you able to figure out how Melissa and Hank's recent deaths fit into this case? Do you think it has anything to do with my dad?" I ask.

"I haven't figured all of that out yet. This is all I have now." He says, while putting his things away.

We sit and talk for a little while about everything and nothing. Anything to get my mind off of the fact that I still have to go back home, which I'm scared to death of doing. Contemplating whether I should reach out to Cryptic. I shouldn't trust him. I don't know him. Between my dad and him, he may be the better of the two.

Times slip away from us, and I've overstayed my welcome. I thank Cory for his time, but before leaving I ask, "Does your mom not like me?"

He studies my face, probably waiting for me to say I'm kidding, but I'm not.

He finally answers, "She doesn't even know you."

Chapter 24: Jason

I have been watching the chat for days but I haven't seen Cory303 or Heath in a while. I gave them a smoking gun, so I'm sure they followed up with it, but they didn't tell the others. They know about my baby girl, Elizabeth, but they think she's in on this. They know about Roman. By now, they have figured out he had dealings that go beyond the coffee shop.

I pack my black bag. Epinephrine, a strong, double-braided rope, a change of clothes, and a knife just in case I need it. I throw on another one of Ian's suits and step into a fresh pair of Tom Fords, picking chestnut this time. Gathering a thick glob of gel, I lather my hair in it until it is heavy from the weight. Then, I brushed it back, exactly how Roman wears his.

Things became clear to me after speaking with Lisa. I've done a job for Roman. I've been punished by Christophe. Tonight, I do another job. I knock two tasks off of my list that belong to two different agendas. One for Roman and one for me. I need to think like Roman, move like Roman. I needed to be that motherfucker.

I button my jacket up, clasping the cuff links around my wrist, and saunter out of Ian's room. The knife is sitting on the counter that I used to slice my steak with. I pick it up, enjoying the happiness of having the feel of the knife in my hand. I take the blade and hold it against my palm, applying pressure on the handle while the blade glides down.

Bright crimson dribbles down, but before making it to my wrist, my tongue darts out, catching every drop. I position my lips in a circular form and begin suctioning, slurping the blood like a newborn does a nipple. Savoring the sweet taste of Ian's internal fluid.

My vision was clearer, colors popped. Posture is erect. My focus is precise. I'm prepared for the encore, but I have a little longer to wait for that. I will settle for tonight, the main performance. Picking up my keys, I headed out of the penthouse to my brand-new Tahoe. The one I recently purchased looks exactly like Roman's.

I may have gone a little crazy. Losing a daughter would do that to you. I drove down the strip on Main Street, running through the plan in my head. Cars line up to be parked by valet. Once it was my turn, I turned to look at the man standing in front of me, awaiting my keys.

"Nice night, sir." He said, tipping his hat to me.

I tossed my keys in his hand and slipped a few dollars into the other.

"Thank you, sir." He spoke while he carefully entered my Tahoe and pulled away.

The vintage home provided high ceilings with patterns of angels engraved. The color pattern included multiple shades of brown and cream-colored paint. I walked down a long dimly lit hallway to the dining area, where I could hear the voices of the people I needed to impress tonight.

As I bent the corner to the entrance, Christophe's voice overpowered the others. He shouts, "Ian, my boy, I'm glad you could make it."

My mouth turned upward into a slight smile. I said, "I wouldn't miss it for the world."

I motioned to grab a seat on the edge of a long, family-style table. Looking around, Roman sat at the head, watching everyone gather and take their respective seats as well.

Roman's eyes landed on mine, taking in my new appearance. He was thinking I'd taken this charade too far or impressed by how much I resembled him and his men. With his eyes never leaving mine, he grabbed a glass and a spoon, tapping them together lightly, but loud enough to get the attention of everyone in the room.

He rose and said, "Good evening everyone, thrilled you could join us." His pearly white teeth were blinding. He continued, "Tonight, we celebrate the efforts of every one of you. Your hard work doesn't go unnoticed. We are preparing a special meal tonight, one you are sure to never forget."

He winks at the guests and continues with his closing statement, "I'm hoping you will enjoy this feast as much as I will. Let's reap the benefits of our success and eat together like comrades."

He thrusts his glass in the air and praises erupt from around the table. Roman takes a seat and I follow suit. Immediately, I feel a hand dart over to me. A sweaty, cold palm encases mine, belonging to none other than Christophe.

"You're good at butchering. Help the others in the kitchen." He whispers, not giving me an option, but an order.

I snatch my hand back, flinging my eyes toward the kitchen. Two butlers stand by the kitchen door holding trays where Champaign rests on top. My eyes fly back to Christophe who is impatiently waiting for me to get the hell up and do what

I'm told.

I flatten out my suit with the palms of my hands, running them down the length of my torso as I stand. My intimidation radiates from all senses. My focus is on the kitchen door as I make my way to what I hope will not cause me to vomit, ruining my chance to complete the task. I push my way into the kitchen while nodding at the butler to my left.

Eyeing the inside, it doesn't take long to realize why Christophe sent me here. Fillet bodies of foreign women hang in the air, dangling from an automatic pulley. Blood trickles down their legs from the sliced-open abdomens, revealing that their internal organs have already been removed. *Their organs are probably sitting on ice somewhere waiting to be sold.*

My stomach churns a little, vomit threatening to erupt. I swallow it down. Chaos ensues as the kitchen staff races around to prepare this ungodly meal. One staff member randomly threw a knife into my chest, demanding that I finish removing meat from the women.

I don't mind a stabby session, but I do mind this. Although the women are already dead, I don't harm the innocent. As I battle with my mind, my feet follow a mind of its own and approach the bodies.

Knife still in hand, I position it on the interior thigh of one woman, applying pressure, neatly carving a deep line down her leg. Blood surges from the laceration and begins boiling on the surface of the skin, bubbling out. My tongue dances in my mouth, but my lips won't part. *Please maintain self-control. Don't let them see you drink the blood of a dead woman.*

Working my magic with the knife, I slice around the top and upper side of the thigh, preparing to remove the quadriceps. The skin flaps down once sliced away from fat and muscle. I stand back to appreciate my work before noticing the blood on my suit.

An hour has passed, and I have removed the meat from both women. I take the knife to my nostril and inhale deeply, refusing to give in to my desires. Although this isn't harming the innocent, they're already dead. I would have regrets knowing I'd consumed the blood of the innocent. The blade rests against my thigh, my hand swiping it away on my pants instead.

Back to my seat at the table, chattering is taking place around me while we all wait for supper to be delivered. Shortly, the door of the kitchen swings open and butlers file out with heaps of meat stacked on top. They sit the trays down in the center of the table one by one and return to the kitchen. Leaving us wrongdoers to feast on a meal that I have hoped will bring Ebola to everyone who partakes.

Trays circulate among us, giving each of us the opportunity to choose what we want. The tray lands in my possession and Roman's eyes strike mine, daring me not to take a piece. I know what I have to do. I take one, forking the smallest piece I can find.

Cutting through the meat, I slice off a bite-size portion of human muscle and place it between my molars. My mouth moved like a sloth, not wanting to taste, not wanting to be satisfied. I grabbed my drink and downed it, the burning liquid taking the flesh with it. I motioned to the butler for more alcohol. It's well-needed.

Chapter 25: Jason

Dinner was over, but I knew staying behind to clean was a task for me to do. I didn't mind. After tonight, that shit will never happen again. The butlers cleaned the table while I disposed of what was remaining of the women we feasted on tonight. Christophe stayed behind to help me or monitor me. Either way, I'm glad he stayed. His presence is much needed for what I have planned.

We took turns taking loads of body parts to the dump van that awaited us outside. Christophe will take it to the landfill later tonight and burn it. The kitchen was spotless by the time we finished, which took hours to do.

"You did great work tonight," Christophe said.

"How long have you worked for Roman?" I ask. I no longer cared if I cross any lines. He was going to die tonight, anyway.

"That's none of your business, boy. If you want to stay in our good graces, you would keep your fucking mouth shut."

"Right. Pop locks on containers of missing people, eat human meat, and keep my fucking mouth shut." I babbled with attitude while pacing around the kitchen.

I purposefully buried my hands deep in my pockets to make me look weak. Christophe doesn't know I'm not Ian. I'm his worst nightmare. The boogeyman is coming to collect tonight.

My face contorts, providing him with a full view of crazy.

Christophe rushes over to me in full force, ready to tackle, but I'm calm. My feet shift out of the way, out of his line of direction, and he runs into the wall. Cursing and spitting out blood, he looks over to me, darkness flooding his face.

Blood oozing through his teeth, he says, "You piece of shit. You're nothing like your father. You're a disappointment."

I laugh, a laugh so loud it could rumble this old house. "Do you think I care what a scumbag has to say about me? You don't remember me, do you? Oh wait, I've never told you who I am."

I continue to pace the room with my hands still in my pockets, ready to spill the truth. Only, he's not who I want to have this conversation with. It should be Roman in his place. So I will give him the simpler version.

The blade flings open while I remove my hands from my pockets.

"I know you're too stupid to think for yourself and you only know how to follow orders," I say while I twirl the blade through my fingers. Christophe watches me with confusion.

I continue, "A few years ago there was a house fire. You were ordered to set my home on fire to give Roman a place where he could build a coffee shop. My home was in the prime location and he wouldn't take no for an answer. I couldn't have been persuaded to move, no matter the amount of money. So he ordered you to burn my home down."

Christophe's eyebrows nearly kiss. He's confused as hell at hearing Jason's story spill from Ian's lips.

"What are you talking about?" Christophe asks, while spitting blood onto the floor from his still bleeding mouth.

"Roman ordered you to burn down Jason Turner's home.

Did he or did he not?" I question, fury building.

"Yea. So what?" Christophe shrugs.

"So, I've risen from the dead, ready to claim my victory." I muse as I watch the blood drain from Christophe's face. He doesn't fully understand the visual of Ian pacing the room, but he knows the story I'm giving him is true.

"What do you plan to do?" He asks.

"Don't worry. You're about to find out." I retaliate.

My feet shift back and forth like I'm in a game of dodgeball. The blade stops twirling in my hand and I bend down to grab the pre-filled syringe out of my black bag, stuffing it in my pocket.

Christophe notices my change in position and sees that as an opportunity to strike. He charges me again, hoping this time to make contact. I've waited too long for this, only to die before getting my hands on Roman. He's closing in on me, but as soon as he gets close enough, I fall to my knees and slide around the bag to the opposite side. Once out of his line of direction, again, he hurls himself into the wall.

In agony, he falls to the ground and in that split second; I straddle him from behind. My left arm wrapped around his forehead, pulling his head back and elongating his neck. I place the knife to his throat and give him the nail in his coffin.

"I died under the bridge alongside Hank 5 years ago. I've lived as Hank, then Melissa, then Ian, and now you. The last person I kill will be Roman because that order not only killed me, but my daughter burned in the fire also. You killed my daughter, Elizabeth, you sick bastard."

Tears trailed down his cheeks after spilling from his eyes. He asked, "Wh-, who are you?"

"I'm Jason Turner". I said, as I sliced his throat.

Blood pooled on the floor as I watched him crawl pathetically, attempting to leave the kitchen. He hoped someone could save him, but no one could save him from me. I withdrew the double braided rope from my bag and positioned it on the pulley that held the women up hours earlier. After tying the knot, I slipped my hand over the handle of the knife and retrieved the syringe from my pocket.

Christophe continued to inch his way to the kitchen door, losing the fight. His battle coming close to an end while his blood pressure tanks from the loss of blood. I place thick towels around his neck after balling them up. The support will both provide pressure so he doesn't bleed out and assist with clotting.

His hands and arms go limp to his side. His pupils dilate and fixate altogether. I slit my throat, Ian's throat, while simultaneously injecting epinephrine into Christophe's thigh.

"See you soon, Chris," I rush the words out before my demise.

The switch was excruciating because of the amount of blood Christophe had lost. His body is weak but has enough strength to finish the job. I scooped up the head of Ian's lifeless body and positioned his neck in the noose. After securing the noose tightly, I hit the up arrow on the automatic pulley. Ian's body rose with the rope, straightening him as his feet hovered over the floor.

I watched as his body hung in the air, swaying like a pendulum. Pulling out a cigarette from Christophe's pocket, I lit it, dragging the thick smoke into my lungs. My work here is done and damn, is it beautiful? I pulled out the Polaroid and snapped a quick photo.

My list was almost to the end, and I could feel the excitement bubble down beneath. I took another drag, exhaling a dark cloud when the sound of movement behind me made it clear someone had joined in on the fun. Not caring to turn around to see whose presence it was. It didn't matter to me.

The presence behind me was motionless and silent. I puffed my cigarette again. A grumble from behind sounded off.

"What the fuck is going on?" said the voice behind me.

I turned with the cigarette dangling from my lips, relaxation resting in my body, facing Roman. His disbelief is astonishing. I offered him no words. Instead, I flicked the cigarette away from me with my fingertips and walked out of the kitchen. I shoulder-bumped Roman with force on my way out, causing him to stumble slightly backward.

"What the hell has gotten into you?" he seethed.

I called back as I continued to walk, "You meant to ask, who the hell has gotten into me?"

Chapter 26: Heather

Roman hasn't been home for a few days and I have been grateful for the lack of presence. After some online searching, thanks to Cory, I went down a rabbit hole of all things related to Dmitri, then all things Roman.

The chat chimed. I began reading the entries in *SpillSecrets*:

MurderEgo: Where has everyone been? Heath never misses a day to update us, yet she's been gone for days.

Me: I'm here.

LunaLunaLuna: Are you okay?

Me: Yes. I'm okay. I just have a lot going on.

LunaLunaLuna: Care to share?

Cory303: Mind your business, Luna. If she wanted you to know, she would have told you by now.

ByteBender: Cory, geez. Calm down.

Cory303: You're right. I'm sorry.

LunaLunaLuna: It's okay.

Me: It's been quiet for a few days. I had nothing to report. Figured we all could use a break from this chat.

MidnightMuse: I don't need a break. This chat is all I look forward to everyday.

MurderEgo: Things haven't been quiet, Heath. You've just been missing out.

Me: What do you mean?

MurderEgo: Not only have you not been in the chat, but you haven't paid attention to the news either?

I turned to face the television, clicking through channels to see what the news outlets were reporting. Nothing but weather, no breaking news surfaced. I turned back to the chat.

Me: I guess I haven't. What did I miss?

Cory303: You missed yesterday's news.

Me: And you didn't tell me?

Cory303: I knew you needed time. Didn't want to bother you.

Me: Someone please tell me what the hell is going on!

LunaLunaLuna: Ian was found dead.

Me: Ian? Cory, my Ian?

Cory303: Yes.

Me: Where? How?

Cory303: They discovered him in the kitchen of an old Victorian home on Main Street.

Me: What was he doing there?

Cory303: Heath, I don't know. He was wearing a suit and covered in blood. Likely attended some party.

Me: When was this? *I wracked my brain. Two nights ago, my dad attended a dinner party in town. Not sure if it was the same party Ian had died at, but I wouldn't be surprised if it was.*

LunaLunaLuna: Two nights ago.

Crap.

Me: Let me guess, he had a slice to the throat as well.

Typing...

Cory303: Yes, but there is something else. He was hanging by a noose.

Me: That's new for our predator. Why slice his throat and

hang him from a noose if he's already dead/dying?

Cory303: Because I told him to…

Me: Are you talking about in the chat when you playfully said something about hanging the victims?

Cory303: Yes. CrypticCrawler wanted to send a message to let us know he's the person committing the murders by using my idea to do it.

MidnightMuse: Or it could just be a coincidence.

LunaLunaLuna: Do you really want to take that chance Midnight?

Me: I think my dad was at the dinner party where Ian died.

Cory303: Why do you think that?

Me: Because he went to a dinner party 2 nights ago, dressed in his tux as always. I wasn't sure if it was the same one, but it makes sense. Cryptic is after my dad, which he told us in this chat. Cryptic also killed Ian. I don't think it is a coincidence he sent us a message by hanging Ian with a rope. Also, I don't think it's a coincidence Ian was killed at the same dinner party my dad attended. He wanted to show us how easily he could get close to Roman.

Typing...

ByteBender: Enough of talking about it. Why don't we just go to the police?

CrypticCrawler: That won't help you.

Typing...

Blank message

Chapter 27: Jason

I kissed my two fingers and placed them on the picture of Ian, now being fully initiated to the corkboard. Three pictures remain. One of Roman, and one of his daughter who has icy, blue eyes and jet-black hair. The one who looks haunted. The last picture is of Christophe. He invited himself to this party. He may already be dead but I'm still living in his body.

I have a meeting with Roman today to explain my recent activities. I don't like the idea of answering to anyone, but being as Christophe was Roman's lapdog, I may as well get familiar with playing the part. His driver is due to pick me up in a few, but not from my storage unit. No one knows I have this unit, and they will not find out today.

I hopped in my Tahoe and drove to Christophe's home. Christophe lives in a quaint neighborhood in a pleasant home wrapped by a white-picket fence. He lives with his wife and two children who were ecstatic to see daddy was home. I gave them light kisses on the cheek. *Which was weird as hell.*

The only reason I came inside was to change into something suitable to meet Roman in. Otherwise, I would have stood outside to wait for the driver. As I'm in the closet, roaming through suits deciding which I would wear today, Christophe's wife is speaking to me from behind in Russian. I have no idea what she's saying, so I smile and nod. Nod and smile. I do this again and again until I'm fully dressed.

Giving her a peck on the cheek, I walk out. Not sure if that's what all the fuss is about or not. She remained quiet in enough time for me to see the driver pull up outside of the fence. Weirdly, I was relieved to trade one nuisance for another.

As I opened the backdoor to claim my seat, I noticed Roman sitting on the other side, waiting for me. "Join us," he mused.

Hair slicked back, he's wearing a tight-fitted jogger suit and loafers. He has on shades today to hide the demonic look in his eyes or to protect his eyes from the sun. Maybe both are true.

I sat as close to the door as possible to avoid touching him. The feel of his skin would trigger me to thrust my fist deep into his throat and rip it out through his mouth. I opted to keep my hands in place, webbed together in my lap.

He began what I knew would be a long line of questioning. He said, "About Ian, I need to understand why you did it."

I studied his face, needing to know whether he was upset or relieved. I'm sure remaining quiet, and not answering his question, is a sign of disrespect. Instead of answering with a statement, I answered with a question. Doing so would probably piss him off, too.

"Should I not have killed him?" I ask.

"Don't play around with me. I don't give a shit about the kid. You choosing to hang him at my dinner party is what I'm referring to."

He swiped a handkerchief from his coat pocket and dabbed the sweat forming around his lips.

I answer, "I had to. He was trying to kill me."

"Kill you? He's a kid. You could have found another way to handle him other than what you did." He held his finger up to me as his phone rang.

He sent it to voicemail.

"You're right. I wasn't thinking clearly." I give in. No sense in going back and forth. I will never win this battle.

"If you feel like hanging Ian was necessary, I trust your judgment. If any of this blows back on me, I'll hang you just like you did Ian." He removes his glasses so I can see the annoyance in his eyes. Then he puts his glasses back on and looks out the window for the rest of the ride.

He will be dead far before he can feel the intensity of the blowback.

We rode in silence for a while until I realized where the driver was taking me. He is taking me to the countryside where Roman's cabin is located. A man like him has to keep many properties available for many reasons.

The port is where he receives shipments of his merchandise. The coffee shop is where he puts on the front of a successful business while laundering money from his illegal one. His cabin is where his men hang out. They stay out of the way and only come when called. That is where they lie low, but that is also where they get rid of bodies. No one will look for you out there.

His home is where he keeps everything clean. He's never to bring anything illegal or any problems to his home. That explains why he's never there. Sure, he's busy, but it's hard keeping illegal activity away from a trafficking lord. His entire existence is illegal.

Roman's phone rings again.

This time he answers, "This is Roman."

He paused for a while, listening to whoever was screaming

on the other end. Pulling the phone away from his face so he wouldn't have to hear, he let them rant. When the line went quiet, he pulled the phone back to his ear and began talking through gritted teeth.

"I don't care who you are. You will watch the way you speak to me. I know how to run my business. If you don't agree with that, why don't you come run it yourself!" he says.

Hands trembling from resentment, he stabs the end button and smashes the phone into the back of the driver's seat. He punches the seat over and over, out of rage until he's out of breath. Watching Roman lose his shit was nice to see. I hope I burried the excitement deep, making sure it's not visible on my face.

He calms down and his body settles. Roman turns to me and stares, not at me, through me. He says nothing, but his mouth part opens and blood spills out. His face turned an ashy white.

I panicked when he coughed, blood spewing into my face and onto my suit. "He needs a hospital. Get him to a hospital now!" I scream at the driver.

"Hey, keep your eyes open, Ro. Focus on me. You're not allowed to die right now." I say, slapping his face.

If he dies now, I'll bring him back just to kill him again.

Chapter 28: Heather

Hospitals are always cold. Some people believe hospitals keep temperatures below freezing to help eliminate germs and bacteria. I think, so many people die in hospitals, that they have to keep their bodies chilled long enough to keep their organs in good condition. My mind is hyper-focused on Roman. I can't think straight. What am I saying?

I shake off the crazy thoughts and step into my father's room. He's awake with a tube in his nose—the tube leading to the wall where a suction container sits. An annoying sound of forced air fills the room, sucking the blood from my dad's stomach into the container.

They poked and prodded his arms, leaving behind two IV accesses in each. They connected both accesses to bags of fluids hanging on a pole. His palms are facing straight up while the backs of his hands lie on the bed. He looks depleted and I've never seen him this weak. Almost makes me want to feel sad for him. Almost.

Christophe sits in the far right corner. His arms and legs gaped open, spread across the chair. His body is relaxed but his head is facing straight ahead, focused. The corner he's settled in is dark, and he's encased in the darkness. His presence is creating a tense feeling, sucking all the oxygen into his black hole.

I mouse, "Hey, Christophe. Thanks for saving my dad."

Despite my kind gesture, the attempt to crack a sincere smile failed because my kindness wasn't reciprocated. Christophe's eyes bore through me, not acknowledging my presence. I turned to walk towards my dad, feeling Christophe's eyes burn a hole in my back.

I lace my fingers with Roman's. His eyes are closed, but he's still breathing according to the monitor.

"Dad?" I spoke. His lids slightly parted, attempting to gain focus.

He blinked a few times before responding, "Heather?"

"I'm here," I assure him while rubbing the side of his arm.

I take a seat next to the bed, casting a look over to where Christophe sits. His focus never leaves me. *What a fucking creep.*

"Are you okay? What happened?" I asked Roman.

"I don't know. One minute I'm talking on the phone, the next I'm coughing up blood. If it wasn't for him." He nodded his head over to Christophe. This time, I didn't look. He continued, "I would be dead."

I glanced over to the canister on the wall, filling up with blood and yellow chunks. I ask, "Where is this coming from?" My gaze pointed to the canister.

"My stomach. The doctor said I had internal bleeding. This tube," he points to the tube in his nose, "is suctioning the blood out of my stomach."

My eyes fall. Hating him was hard to do while seeing how vulnerable he was. However, his vulnerability creates the perfect time to get what I need. Information.

I let my diarrhea of the mouth get the best of me. The words spill out on their own. "Why are you never home?"

He looks over at me, this time completely focused. "What do you mean?"

"You're never home. Is it because of the coffee shop? Please don't lie to me."

I could see him glance at Christophe, who I could hear shift in the chair behind me. *Does this make you uncomfortable creep?*

"Heather, baby, don't ask questions you don't want to know the answers to." He warns.

I counter, "What if I already know the answers?"

"What if you 'think' you know, but truly, you don't? If you open this can of worms, you will regret it."

Ignoring his warning, I continue with the questions. "The port. Is that where you are most of the day, receiving your shipments?"

His hands ball into bloodless fists, wanting to smash something. He's pissed, I know. What did he expect? That I would remain the little, naive girl he has always known me to be?

I see him cast another look in the corner and ask, "Would you like Christophe to leave so we can talk?" My attitude was getting the best of me. Knowing Roman couldn't do anything about it only made matters worse.

"I'm not going anywhere," Christophe says through gritted teeth.

I turn to face him, raising my voice, "Who asked you?"

Christophe stands, baring his teeth. An ugly scar, beefy-red in color, comes into full view as he towers over me. *Ian had the same scar on his neck at the coffee shop.*

Roman yells, "Sit down, Heather. You're not thinking clearly."

I do as I'm told while turning to Roman. "I'm thinking clearer than I ever have. Tell me about your organ business."

Christophe sits back down and positions himself in the seat behind me. He doesn't intend to remove himself and mind his own business. I just pretend he's no longer around.

Roman doesn't speak. I'm sure he's still processing my revelation. Irritated with his silence, I pull out my laptop, mindlessly signing onto *SpillSecrets*. Immediately, the messages chime.

LunaLunaLuna: I hope Heath's okay.

MidnightMuse: I'm sure she's fine. She's a tough girl.

LunaLunaLuna: How would you know?

MidnightMuse: I don't. Just trying to make you feel better.

Cory303: Heath, please give us an update on you, not your dad.

ByteBender: What do you have against her dad? Are you just set out not to like anyone?

MurderEgo: Heath, your dad is all over the news. We know he's in the hospital. Just let us know you're okay.

I typed, but Roman's voice interrupted my train of thought. "What is on your computer that has your attention?"

"What is at the port that has yours?" My head cocks to the side, challenging him.

"I will tell you when I'm ready. Right now isn't a good time."

"Okay, Dmitri." I call him, hitting below the belt.

He fumes, "What the fuck did you just call me?"

A roar of laughter erupts from behind. Christophe proves his inability to control his amusement.

Chapter 29: Jason

Heather begs Roman for information, but he can't stand to share in front of me. He also isn't in the position to ask me to leave. I remain calm in the corner, providing a dangerous amount of discomfort to everyone in the room.

Seeing Roman vulnerable makes it difficult to keep my desires at bay. It would be too easy to kill him now, which is the only thing saving him. I don't prefer my prey wounded. I want a challenge. Heather will receive the answers, whether he wants to give in willingly or if I have to make him. She doesn't know that yet.

She may have liked Christophe before, but I can tell she doesn't feel comfortable around the new version of me. I'm scared to speak because I can't control what may leave my lips. Roman's hospitalization was unexpected. Saving the man who murdered my daughter, well, that could only mean hell froze over.

I know why I did it. I had to. The vision of him dying under my blade is all I've dreamed of for years. He doesn't get off easy because of something petty like internal bleeding. I scoff. That's just not going to work for me.

I shift around uncomfortably, making a loud, unnecessary noise to remind Heather and Roman of my presence. Also, to remind them, I'm not leaving. I refuse to leave this hospital and I refuse to leave Roman's side. He's come too close to death for my comfort. I'll take good care of him until I say he can die.

The visions of my house burning have haunted me for years. The sounds of my daughter's screams have pierced my soul for years. My nightmares interrupt the need for sleep, exhausting me. Now, I have the control. Now I'm the hunter. The shadow in the dark.

I don't body hop because I want to. I have to. Being incognito to the people I seek revenge on gives me the greatest satisfaction. Existing right under their noses and haunting them in the flesh is a gift that keeps on giving.

A nurse enters the room and introduces herself with a bag of blood in her hand. I swipe my sweaty palms on my pants, trying to maintain my sanity. Sweat forms at my hairline as she passes by me with a bag that I want to snatch from her grasp and down like a glass of whiskey.

I've never had the desire to consume blood when I was myself, as Jason. My first body hop, when I became Hank, is when the desire ignited. I chalked it up to the thirst for gore being a side effect. The feeling I get from injecting epinephrine during a switch doesn't come close to the adrenaline I gain from feeding off of the bodies I embody. My existence is based on adrenaline. Without it, I may as well wither away.

Knowing blood is a lifeline makes me feel powerful while drinking it. Gives me a godly feeling that no other drug can deliver. I don't crave blood, but when it's in my presence, I want a taste. The act of ingesting vital fluid allows me to feel alive when everything else about my existence is dead.

The nurse carries the pack of red blood cells over to the IV pole, sliding the pre-filled tubing into a warmer. My eye twitches and tremors form in my hands. Heather notices but says nothing. I'm sure she's afraid to acknowledge me.

My eyes follow the blood as the nurse sets the pump to infuse, and the crimson flows into Roman's veins. Once in his body, my desires fade. Digesting any part of him disgusts me. My body settles and I release a long breath.

The nurse leaves after making sure Roman doesn't have a reaction to the infusion. I would have sworn she knew I would snap her neck if he died. My relaxed state puts the mood at ease.

Rosie's entrance bursts the bubble, and we are back at square one. Only this time, I wish I had popcorn for the shit that's about to ignite.

"Daddy, we have a problem," Rosie says while panting.

Her hair is in disarray. Mascara leaks down her face, smudged by the flow of tears. She appeared defeated, slumping her shoulders over. I take her in. Icy, blue eyes with jet-black hair that provide a striking contrast.

Roman shoots a look over to me and I stand, understanding what his look meant.

"I'll handle it," I say, while grabbing Rosie by the arm and leading her out of the hospital room.

She has no fucking idea what she just walked into.

Chapter 30: Heather

I've never seen my sister that terrified. Everything is falling apart and I don't know why. The comments Cory made filtered through my head: *Do you want to continue sitting up in this pretty little house, typing on your pretty little blog, spilling everyone's business while being oblivious to your own?* I wish he wasn't right.

My focus on the lives of others made me negate my life. I barely leave the house. Constantly ignoring my issues, I immerse myself in the problems of other people. I feel bad for myself. How pathetic my existence is. The only people who look forward to hearing from me are the people on my blog. People I barely know. Whose lives are probably just as pathetic as mine.

I stare at the tiles beneath my feet. Roman noticed my discomfort. He wants to console me, but he doesn't know how. I can't help but laugh at how surreal this moment is. The laughter started as slow chuckles, then transitioned into uncontrollable belly-gripping cackles.

I'm certain that Roman's face displays confusion, but the wetness in my eyes makes it difficult to see. Tears stream down my face as I try to gain control. I lean over to the hospital bed for support, completely drained, now questioning my mental health.

I settle and gather my thoughts. "Tell me about your organ business. I will get up and walk out of here if you refuse. This is your last chance." I demand in a serious tone.

"I took over the business when Dmitri went to prison." He admits.

"How did he get caught?"

"Police surrounded the port after Dmitri accepted a shipment. Someone tipped them off." He reminisced.

"Do you know who called it in?"

"It was someone inside the organization. We took care of it." His arms tensed up, showcasing his toughness.

I already know what he means by 'took care of it.' There's no need to get clarification.

"Dmitri went to prison and you just what? Took over?"

"Exactly. I had no choice. I'm Dmitri's only son. I knew it would pass down to me." He sounds regretful. I'm not sure if it's because of the state that he's in or if the abduction of women and children bothers him.

He continues, "I try not to think about the merchandise." *Women and children are not objects.* "That's how I make money, how I make a living. How else will I gift you nice things?"

"I don't care about that. What if I wanted you to get out?" I quiz.

His eyes slit, "There is no getting out."

A loud sigh leaves my lips. So this is it. A family trafficking business sounds perfect for my resume. A thought crosses my mind, itching to leave my lips.

"Since you don't have a son, who will you pass the business down to?"

"I'm already grooming my replacement, Heather. Don't worry. It's not you." He chuckles. After a brief pause, the seriousness returns to his voice. "I need you to know something."

He cusps my hand with both of his, being mindful of his infusions. My breathing shallows, fearing what's coming. My mouth dries as I wonder what the next bomb will be.

He licks his lips and slowly speaks. "This-" he releases one of his hands and twirls a finger around the air in circles, "this is bigger than me and you. I don't make all the rules. I'm just a puppet in this circus. You may think I'm a terrible man right now and that's rightfully so, but I have to answer to someone, too. There's no way I can run an international organ trafficking business alone."

He pauses and returns his hand to mine. "I know you exalted me. Probably thinking what everyone is, that I'm some hero of the community. That I'm here to save people, donate money, and smile for the cameras. That's who I want to be, but that's not the cards life dealt. For that, I'm sorry."

I pull my hand away from his, trying to understand where all of this is coming from. The pump beeps, prompting the nurse to come in. Grateful for the distraction, I locate my computer.

Private chat with Cory303:

Cory303: Heath, I have something you need to see. Please respond to this message asap.

Me: Hey Cory, what is it?

Cory303: I think I've found our guy. I've found Cryptic.

Chapter 31: Jason

Rosie is a ball of nerves, tremors infesting her body. I offer her no remorse. We sit in the visitor's lobby for hours in silence. I take in every piece of movement around me. Soaking in the slightest activity: the sound of a nurse clicking her pen, a baby sucking her bottle, or the piercing sound of the turn of a page in a magazine. I take it all in.

I clock two of Rosie's men follow us from the room to the lobby with ample distance between. They try to blend in, not making it obvious who they are. I'm not stupid. I know who Rosie is, and I know why they're here to protect her.

Rosie plays a vital part in the intricate pieces of this puzzle. From the outside looking in, it could be hard to tell. She's young, fierce, easy to be mistaken for a normal, hormonal teenager. That's what makes her a perfect fit, like a lock and a key.

Unfortunately for Heather, she never notices why Rosie is never home. She thinks Rosie is constantly away to shop for clothes to wear when she's hanging out. Sometimes, she brings home garments to Heather as a gift for being away. Like father, like son, I mean daughter.

Her eyes well with tears, but she's holding them back. Her dad taught her well. She's attempting to provide a strong front, not showing any signs of weakness. Especially in front of her men and me. I would love nothing more than to see her pay, to see the pupils in her haunted eyes fixate permanently, but now isn't her time. I can't leave Roman, and for what I have in store, it needs to unfold perfectly.

Her voice deflated, she says, "I've never had to do this alone. I always had Roman by my side to guide me. The men don't respect me. I feel like I've bitten off more than I can chew."

I sit silently, listening to her problems as though I truly care. I don't. She's worried about these niggling issues when her deadliest obstacle is sitting right next to her. Roman had no choice but to appoint Rosie. Heather, being as naïve as she is, would get herself killed the first day.

Rosie had the respect of the men when Roman was there to back her. With him weak in a hospital bed, things need to be set in order. As Christophe, Roman's right hand, the only logical way to restore things would be for me to step up. I'm conflicted.

"Don't leave," I say. "I'll be right back."

I push past the obvious, not-so-obvious bodyguards to make my way outside. The double glass doors to the hospital slide open, and I'm accepted by the darkness. I turn to see Rosie through the glass windows, still sitting in a chair in the lobby, rendered speechless.

Pulling out the burner with one contact, I make the call.

"Lisa?" I ask. She doesn't like to speak first just in case someone else gets a hold of the burner.

Finally, she answers, "Yes?"

"I have to leave Roman for a while, keep an eye on him for me, will you?"

"Leave him?" She questions.

"Just for a bit. Rosie had a hiccup and needed some help."

"What are you doing helping Rosie? First, you save Roman from death and now you're going to help Rosie with what?" She pauses. "Let me guess, organ trading?"

"It's not like that. I know what I'm doing."

"I sure hope so. Don't get too deep into this." Her response is sincere.

"I'll try not to. Christophe would have stepped up. I have to do my part right now. You know that."

"Yeah, well, Christophe wasn't a part of the plan." She scoffs.

I sink. I know that. She always tells me what I don't want to hear. That's her job, though. That's why I depend on her.

"I know, Lisa. So you'll monitor him for me? Make sure no one kills him before I do."

"You know I'll do it for you, Jason. Hurry. Get this over with."

"I will, I promise." I speak truthfully.

"Good. You don't break promises." She says before the line goes dead.

I hope I'm playing this right. Getting in bed with dangerous people. Now I have to show my face, creating the illusion of the head of Clairville's organ trade. Even only temporarily, I didn't want this.

Visions of Elizabeth flash in my memory like an old celluloid film. Her laughing and smiling gives me hope. The sound of her voice calling me 'Dad' created a fire under my ass to stop sulking and get down to business.

I slap my cheeks a few times, fix my button-down, and waltz back into the hospital. I reclaim my spot next to Rosie. Facing my body toward her, I ask, "What do you need me to do?"

She looks up at me with those haunted eyes, hope distilled in them. "Meet the men at the cabin tomorrow night to go over the plan. Another shipment is due in a few days, and they don't trust me enough to tell them how this will go."

She turns away from me and continues, "They trust you, though."

Sure, I'll do it, but it's going to be done my way.

Chapter 32: Heather

Shortly after Christophe and Rosie left the hospital, I did the same. Roman is in excellent hands there. If he's not, oh well. That's his problem.

I parked my Range Rover outside of Starbucks. Waiting far too long for Cory to show, I entered the coffee shop, glancing toward our normal table. Cory already has both of our normal drinks ordered and waiting for me. I walk over and take a seat.

"Didn't see your car outside," I said with a sigh.

"It's in the shop. I drove my mom's." He says while handing me a cold brew.

"What do we have?" I ask.

"You mean, what do I have?" He chuckles. "There is a unit downtown that I believe belongs to our guy."

"You believe? How so?" I question.

"When I come to you with information, it's usually more than just a hunch." His eyebrow raises.

His attention turns to the computer sitting in front of him, fingers chomping down on the keys. I take a few sips of my cold brew, annoyed with Cory's sass and confidence. Granted, he may be a little arrogant sometimes, a Mr. know-it-all, but he does come with receipts to back up his queries. Cory would probably make a better journalist than I ever could. His abilities to hack and find backdoors to retrieve information play highly in his favor. Maybe I should have taken a few geek classes.

He turns his computer screen toward me, and it reveals the unit's information. I lean in to get a better view.

Lisa Hollingsworth.

Unit E17.

Lease date: August 5, 2020. Five years ago.

Account: Active.

Sparks should fly by now. Realization not settling in because Cryptic isn't a woman. If she was, I would see Elizabeth's name on the unit, not Lisa's. I sip more of my drink, waiting for Cory to spill. He's dragging this out, holding back on the information to see the anticipation eat at me.

He points at the name on the screen. He asks, "Lisa doesn't ring a bell for you?"

"Is it supposed to? I know many people by that name, so why don't you get on with it?" I fiddled with the tips of my hair, lacing the red strands between my fingers.

He shifts the computer from between us and removes his glasses. His green eyes and freckles come into full view without the bulk of his glasses to hide them. He holds out his hand to me. I don't grab it because what the hell is he doing?

"I guess I should formally introduce myself. We never properly met outside of the chat. I'm Cory Hollingsworth. Nice to meet you, Heather."

I shake his hand automatically, the customary notion instilled in my muscle memory. Finally, the sparks fly. Lisa Hollingsworth is Cory's mother. The one I met after admiring the scribbled wall in his home. The questions flowed in, but Cory saved himself from the interrogation.

"The unit belongs to my mom. She has a lot on her plate with my brothers and sisters, but something else has been distracting her lately. I found the bill for her unit in the mail after they piled up in our mailbox." He moved the computer between us again and placed his glasses back on his face, positioning them to sit comfortably on the bridge of his nose.

He continues, "I didn't know she had a storage unit. Curiosity is in my nature. Therefore, naturally, I went to check it out, hoping to find something interesting. I found more than what I bargained for."

"What you found in the unit has something to do with Cryptic?"

"It has everything to do with Cryptic."

"So, what's in it?"

"I would rather you see for yourself." His voice trails off. The sound of his laptop closing rings in my ears as he stands from the seat. He tucks his laptop in the pit of his arm and extends the other arm out to me. "I'll take you."

"Cory, I'm scared." My voice trembles.

"You should be," he says, encasing my hand in his as we walk out of Starbucks.

Chapter 33: Heather

I follow Cory to SafeSpace Storage. I park alongside him and wiggle out of the truck. My legs defy me, going weak, making it hard to close the space between Cory and me.

Cory rounds his car and asks, "You okay?"

"I'm doing the best I can. Being a hacker and all, you know how to pick locks too?" I ask with a chuckle. My corny comment brings a little light to the situation.

"No need to pick the lock when I have the key." He holds up a brass key that twinkles in the moonlight. "You need to get yourself together because I don't want you passing out on me. Being a hacker and all, I don't know how to save your life."

He doesn't laugh, he's serious. I don't find humor in it either; I believe him. My conclusion would depend on what I find behind the roll door.

Cory leads me to unit E17 and I grab at his shirt. I fist a ball of the garment in my hand while he positions the key. The clicking of the locking mechanism sounds off and he removes it from the roll door. The lock with the key still intact, placed snuggly in his pocket. He bends slightly with the end of his shirt still in my grasp and plants his hands flush against the door. With pressure, he slides the door up, high enough for us to enter.

Nothing comes into view since the unit is pitch black. We step inside and Cory turns to roll the door down slightly, keeping a crack still visible underneath. I turn with him, scared to let go. I follow his movements in the dark, my foot bumping into what sounds like a cardboard box. *Please don't step on a dead body. Please don't step on a dead body.*

Cory's footsteps halt and I shudder, waiting for the worse to happen. Waiting to feel warm blood oozing down to where my hand grips his shirt from his beheading. That didn't happen, thankfully. Instead, a light screeching sound rips through the darkness.

Cory finishes twisting the lightbulb into its holder until it is snug, and the unit illuminates. I release the fist around his shirt and scan the unit, turning my body in a complete circle to take it all in.

"I know it's a lot to take in." Cory's voice was sincere.

I didn't respond. I couldn't. My lips parted as I mentally agreed with Cory. This is certainly Cryptic's lair. A worn-out bed sits in the corner. Cardboard boxes line the unit's walls. A small, bulky television sits on a round wooden table that can be seen from the bed. Under the table, there is a miniature black refrigerator. One wooden chair accompanies the round table.

I stumble over to the cardboard boxes, where I rummage through them. Men's clothes are balled up and stuffed in each box. I rummaged through a few before getting to a box that held a few pieces of women's clothing. Amidst the clothing is a scarf with blood splattered on it.

I lay the scarf across the palms of my two hands and turn to face Cory. I ask, "Do you think this was Melissa's?"

"That's a very strong possibility." He answers.

I throw the scarf to the side and take in the corkboard behind Cory. I shift past him, softly pushing him to the side. The view in front of me takes what little breath I have left in me. Pains in my stomach form, feeling like someone shoved a dull knife into my abdomen and refused to stop twisting it. Heat rips through me, fury building.

A photo of Roman sits at the top of the board, a photo bigger than the rest that is tacked beneath. A long strand beneath Roman's photo connects him with a photo of my sister, Rosie. I've always loved her icy blue eyes. Although eerie, they were beautiful to me.

My eyes fall to a picture of Hank, which has an x drawn through it. Melissa's Polaroid picture touching Hanks, also with an x drawn through it. Next is a photo of Ian with lines of the same fashion as the others. An x. Resting sloppily on the board is a photo of Christophe. His picture isn't a Polaroid, but a photo that anyone could easily find of him online.

My fingers trace the board, wondering what these people have in common. Without removing my gaze, I speak to Cory behind me. "Christophe's photo doesn't have an x on it."

Cory responds, "I think he's next on the list."

I pull out my phone to snap a picture of the board. My finger trembles while pressing the white button at the bottom of the screen to capture a photo. The sound of the roll door bangs loudly, and a deep voice rumbles through the unit. He hisses, "Delete that."

Our heads snap in unison toward the voice of the figure standing under the roll door. The darkness lines his body. As I look down, I can't help but notice his Tom Fords. *My dad's favorite.* My gaze trails up his slacks to his button-up shirt. I trail my gaze until they meet the scar on his neck and land on his snarky face.

It's the face identical to the photo that rests sloppily on the corkboard. It's Christophe, the next person on Cryptic's list. *What the hell is he doing here?*

Chapter 34: Jason

I'm going to kill Lisa for being so careless. Cory has been a pain in my ass since I introduced myself on the blog. Now he's standing in my storage unit with a shit-eating grin on his face. *Does this little prick not fear me?*

They stood staring at me for longer than I was comfortable with. All of my items surrounding them. I noticed that someone had thrown around the boxes of clothes.

Before letting my presence known, I waited outside while they went snooping. Thankfully, I walked in just in time to see Heather taking a picture of my board. Granted, I don't care if she knows who is on the list. I already told her about wanting Roman. I just don't want her to share the details of my plan prematurely.

Once they realized I was standing at the door, Heather looked at me like she was going to have a seizure. I would have let her, too. I might have laughed a little, watching her twitch on the floor.

We stand for a little while longer in awkward silence. I ponder on what to do. Do I tell the truth, the whole truth, and nothing but the truth? Or do I lie, play my part as Christophe, leaving them to find out later?

Finally, Heather speaks, "What are you doing here?" The

tone of her voice sounds childish. However, I could tell she attempted to put some authority in her voice. It's not working well in her favor.

"Come again?" I muse while approaching her slowly but steadily. She steps backward, almost stumbling on a cardboard box behind her.

"I will not hurt you." I say.

Her sidekick pipes up, "How do we know that?"

I shot a nasty look in his direction. "You don't."

His eyes widen, and he tries to hide it by looking down at his feet.

I position myself in front of Heather, who was cowering before me. "Did you find what you were looking for?"

Tears leak from her eyes. As soon as they fall, she wipes them away swiftly. I sidestep her to grab a napkin. Her body tensed, but I was serious when I said I'm not here to hurt them. They're innocent and I don't hurt the innocent. I hand her a napkin, but she freezes, scared to accept anything from me.

"It's just a napkin, Heather. Take it. It's obvious that you need it." I demand. Seeing her break down in front of me pokes holes in my darkness. She's almost the age my daughter would have been. I wouldn't want to see Elizabeth this way.

"Why are you here?" she blubbers.

My confliction is still present. For the first time, I'm not sure what to do. So I do the only thing I know how when in this situation. I answer with a question. "Why are you here?"

"We are looking for someone." Cory speaks up, realizing Heather isn't in a condition to speak for herself.

"Looking for who?"

"Someone who goes by the online name of Cryptic."

I already knew the answer, but I didn't want them to know I

knew.

"And how did you find this place?" I question.

Cory answers, "It's my mom's unit. I have every right to be here. I can't say the same for you."

There it is. That smart mouth and those snarky remarks is why I don't care for Cory. Although he reminds me a bit of myself, that doesn't mean I enjoy the taste of my own medicine.

"Your mom?" I quiz. I also know Lisa is his mom, and she's the reason he found this unit because she was being careless. Again, I act like I don't know.

"Ugh. Yes, my mom's unit. Why are you here? Did you follow us?"

"I'm not sure how to answer that." I speak truthfully because I don't know how to answer it. If I tell them everything, who's to say they won't leave this unit and tell Roman? If I don't, they will continue to poke and pry until they figure it out on their own. Cory, being Lisa's son, puts me at a great disadvantage.

I would have been more prepared if I would have known sooner who Cory303 was. There are plenty of people by that name. When I saw his name on the blog, I just assumed it was a different Cory. What were the odds?

"Take a seat on the bed. Both of you." I say in a soft tone.

Heather speaks, "What do you plan on doing to us?" She wraps her arms around her torso to protect herself. That lets me know what she's thinking. I could never.

"Heather, I'm not a pervert or a rapist. Look around, there's nowhere else to sit. Either sit on the bed if you want answers or leave." She must be mistaking me for Melissa. *Okay, that was low, even for me.*

They take their positions on the bed, and I take mine on the wooden chair. I position the chair in front of them, preparing for my interrogation. Ready to spill everything.

"I know you both have some questions. I am prepared to answer. There is just one request." I state.

"What is it?" Cory asks.

"This conversation doesn't leave the unit. It is between us. I've worked extremely hard to get to where I am and I will kill anyone who threatens to take this revenge away from me." They snap their heads toward each other when I said the word 'revenge.' I continue, "That last statement includes the both of you." Their bodies go tense while I swing my finger between the two.

I lean forward in the chair, placing my elbows on my knees. My eyes focus on Heather as I say, "My condition is this: you are not to tell your friends on *SpillSecrets* about anything we share here tonight."

Heather eyes me, her mind racing. "How do you know about my blog?"

"Aside from the fact that it is a public blog," I roll my eyes, "I'm the guy you're looking for."

I lean back in the chair holding my arms open like I'm on the cross, "I'm CrypticCrawler."

Chapter 35: Jason

The response they gave me was not the response I was looking for. I was hoping they would yell, scream, or cry, anything other than laugh. I'm uncertain why, but the laughter pissed me off. Maybe it was because I viewed it as disrespectful.

I rose from my chair with force. The backs of my legs tipped the chair over, causing it to fall to the ground, making a loud thud. The laughter halted and the response I was looking for initially finally showed its face.

I slipped a knife out of my pocket, letting it dance between my fingers as I always do. The performance gets their attention, making them uncomfortable. My arms pull back and snap forward like a rubber band, hurling the knife into the wall of the unit. Landing directly between their heads. Their faces warped, and I knew from that moment forward, they would give me their undivided attention.

I moved toward them, causing their bodies to freeze, as if stilling would make them invisible. Leaning in, I grabbed the knife from the wall and stuck it in my pocket. Back at the chair, I picked it up and positioned myself as I was before.

Completely relaxed, I say, "Now, ask me anything."

Cory, who has more balls than Heather, speaks up, "How do we know you're Cryptic?"

I speak, "Let's start from the beginning. I will tell you everything about me and who I've been leading up to becoming, Christophe."

"What do you mean becoming Christophe?"

"Damn, this is going to be a long night." I roll my eyes. "My name is Jason Turner."

Their hands clasp together. Cory gasps while Heather nearly chokes on her own breath. I watch as Cory relaxes. Probably because he thinks I'm lying, and he's prepared to ask me something stupid. I don't let him.

I explain, "I know it's hard to believe because I'm sitting in front of you as Christophe. Before I explain my life story, let me ask you this:" I stand from my seat again, only this time, smoothly. My head shifts back, exposing my scar. "You see this scar around my neck?" No one answers, so I continue, "You remember this same scar on Ian's neck?"

The blood in their hands is ashen from how tight they're holding onto each other. I walk over to the corkboard and remove the pictures with x's on them. Once within arm's reach of Heather, because I don't care a lot for Cory, I hand the photos to her. Again, she's reluctant to accept, but eventually, she does.

"Inspect those photos. Look at their necks. What do they have in common?"

I don't give her a chance to answer verbally because I can see the realization on her face. I continue, "Hank, slit to the throat. Melissa has a slit to the throat. Ian, slit to the throat." I take my index finger and put it up to my neck, mimicking how I'm going to slit my throat when it's time. "You get the idea."

Heather pushes back on her heels, crawling backward in the bed. Her backside touches the wall, and she curls up, bringing her legs to her chest. She folds her arms around her legs, tucking her chin between the knees. She's terrified and I would be too.

"I told you I wouldn't hurt either of you." I said, but my words did not provide her any comfort.

"You've killed people. How could I trust you?" She asks.

"I've only killed people who deserved to die. Everyone on this board deserved what they got." Anger bolted through me temporarily. I decided instead of scaring them with my anger, offering them an explanation may work best.

"Let's begin with Melissa. I killed her because she raped Logan. She was hired to babysit him, but exploited an innocent soul." Heather's wet eyes gazed up at me. I continued, "I killed Ian because he helped your father in the organ trade business."

Heather asked, "What about Hank?"

"Right, Hank." I paced back and forth, wondering where to start. "Hank never had a future, and I'm certain he knew that. He would do anything for scraps of cash. He's the reason Melissa became a drug addict. She was hammered one night while babysitting Logan." I gathered myself. I hate this part. "You know the rest. He played a hand in Logan's rape. Although not directly, that was enough for me to kill him and I would do it all over again."

Heather's jaw dropped, and I continued, "Shortly after, they got a divorce. Melissa continued to live in that shack she called home and Hank ended up homeless. He slept under the bridge and begged for money until I came along."

Cory shifted on the bed, still not fully convinced. He asked, "So how did you become Hank? How are you claiming to be Jason when I'm looking at the body of Christophe? That's not physically possible."

"I knew this would come. However, it is possible. I was

supposed to die in the house fire. Technically, I died. My body suffered severe burns, but I escaped and only made it as far as the bridge. Hank was dying too, overdosing on drugs. A bystander called 911 after seeing me lying on the ground covered in smut. When EMS came, we were both near death. I had no chance of survival, but Hank had a chance. They injected him with Narcan, which he responded to. Shortly after his heart stopped, so did mine."

I turned to look at them, making sure they were paying attention. This next part is important. "We died at the same time. EMS started CPR on Hank, injecting him with epinephrine. After a few rounds, I woke up in Hank's body. Our souls left together, but my soul found its way back to the body that would give it life."

Heather finally found the courage to speak. "So, is that how you've been becoming other people? By killing them and killing yourself, hoping your soul will make it to their body?" I could tell she was confused and not completely sold on the truth.

Cory rubs his hand down her arm to console her and directs his next words to me. "I think I can provide a better explanation."

Exclusive Chapter: Cory

I know Christophe isn't who is standing before me. I know it's Jason. I knew all along.

I found out my dad was alive when he came to Lisa after the fire as Hank. He could have appeared as anyone, and I would have known it was him. A different appearance, a unique voice, none of it matters. Certain things will never change, no matter what body you're in or how many people you become. The way he walked, his posture, and how he spoke about me all gave it away. Seeing him now, passionate about his revenge for me, is an undeniable sign that he's my father.

When he appeared at Lisa's doorstep, I hid in the hallway to listen. He didn't care about himself; he was only concerned about his daughter, about me. Standing out of their line of sight, I watched as he cried in her arms, mourning my death. I wanted to say something, something like, "Dad, I'm here" but I couldn't. I refrained from telling him because I was terrified he wouldn't believe me. Even I wouldn't believe me. I would have had to explain how I took over Cory's body just as he's trying to explain how he does it. It sounds crazy and impossible. I kept my mouth shut.

Lisa knew I wasn't her son. It didn't take long for her to realize. The things I did, her son never would. I was a sassy, snarky female in a male's body. Mother's just know and her intuition was right.

I came clean to her and proved her suspicions were correct. That is when I learned about astral projection. Souls can detach their bodies when they're in a deeply relaxed state. They can travel into other bodies that are no longer inhabited by another spirit. Things made sense.

Cory was obsessed with astral projecting. So obsessed that he did it regularly once he figured out how to control his spirit. He astral projected the night I was dying in the fire. I could feel the detachment while my body burned. My soul found a body that still had a beating heart. I didn't take it on purpose.

When I woke up as Cory, my first feeling was confusion. I was completely clueless about projection and body switching. I simply got lucky. After a while, depression settled in. It was difficult being female in a male's body. It was hurtful knowing I couldn't have my old body back. I had to learn to be Cory, to live a new life with new people. None of it was easy.

After my spiritual lesson, Lisa and I agreed not to tell my dad. He had a plan to seek revenge for my death and I didn't want to stand in the way of that. I knew that if he suspected I was alive, living as someone else, it would discourage him from his plan. I want Roman dead as much, if not more, than my dad does. He stole our lives away from us.

Harboring this secret has been the hardest thing I've ever done. Watching my dad mourn me and spiral out of control haunted me more than my death in the fire. We were so close physically, yet so far apart.

Lisa signed the lease at SafeSpace storage for a unit on behalf of Jason, under her name. To give him a place to stay and lie low while he perfects his plan. I would visit him, keeping a safe distance to avoid being noticed.

I knew every step of his plan because Lisa told me. She gave me updates as she received them. I found *SpillSecrets* and knew it was the perfect opportunity to build a relationship with Heather.

I've been feeding her bits and pieces of CrypticCrawler, not to give too much away too soon. She never questioned how I knew as much as I did. I'm sure she chalked it up to my hacking abilities.

The day I get to tell him who I truly am, that I'm Elizabeth, will be the best day of my life. That day will be my second chance. I'll get to resume the life I had with my father again. Which is why I want this to end soon. I can't hold on to this secret for much longer.

Chapter 37: Jason

Cory explained the process of astral projection in a way I never could. Either he did his homework or he was babbling off a pile of bullshit. His theory on how I'm able to trade bodies offered more reasoning than my explanation did.

We took a brief recess, walking around the unit in silence. They needed time to digest the information before hearing more. I offered them bottles of water from my mini fridge. They gladly took it, consuming every drop. The revelations rendered them speechless and thirsty.

After they resumed their positions on the bed, I knew it was time for more lines of questioning. I stood in front of them, preparing to answer anything they wanted to know.

Heather asked, "Tell me the story of why you want to kill Roman. I need to hear it from you."

I removed a cigarette from Christophe's pocket, lighting the tip. The end crackled and burned as I drew in smoke. Pacing, I took a few draws before answering her question. I spoke. "Roman approached me once. I was home with my daughter, Elizabeth, when I heard a knock on my door." Cory shifts on the bed at the sound of my daughter's name. His eyes softened for the first time since this conversation started. "The first time we spoke, he was nice, asking if there was any amount of money he could offer me for the location of my home."

I took a few more draws, letting out a black cloud of smoke. "Over time, he became impatient, and forceful. He gave me an ultimatum. Either I could take the money and find somewhere else to live, or he would force me out." I took one last drag and put the fire out on the wooden table, creating a circular burn in the wood.

"I knew Roman was a dangerous guy. I knew he took over the organ trade from his dad, therefore, I knew what he was capable of. It didn't matter. I would never uproot my daughter's life for someone else's gain. I stood my ground," I said.

Walking over to the bed, I leaned over, reaching under the pillow to retrieve one last photo. My pacing continued as I concentrated on the Polaroid in my hand. "My daughter was comfortable in that home. We lived there together as a family when her mom was still alive." My voice cracked when the thoughts of my wife came to the forefront. "I wasn't moving for that bastard, but he delivered on his promise, sending Christophe to light my home on fire. Roman didn't know Elizabeth was home that night. She was supposed to be away at camp. She came down with a stomach bug. I canceled her trip to camp with the promise that she could go the following year."

I sat a picture of my daughter on the bed, between Heather and Cory, and they both stared at the picture in awe. A river of tears stream from Cory's eyes. His attempts to swipe them away as they fell failed. I offered him a napkin and continued, "Christophe began the fire downstairs in the living room. By the time I woke, because of the smell of smoke, there was a fierce blaze inching its way upstairs. The house's structure blocked our exits off. It was close to giving in. There was no way I could make it to my baby girl. Her screams still haunt me, breaking my heart repeatedly every time I think of it." I retrieved a napkin for myself, wiping tears of my own.

"Roman got what he wanted, the ability to build his coffee shop in a prime location. On top of my daughter's final resting place. If it wasn't for Cory's mom, Lisa, I wouldn't be here. She rents this unit in her name for me. I owe my life to her." The tears stop falling. I gather myself, hoping they've heard enough.

Heather said, "I'm sorry Jason. My family has done a lot of wrong. I promise not to say a word. Turns out, I don't break my promises either." She cracks a smile and I know she's referencing what I said in her blog.

For the first time, Cory is speechless. He doesn't give any snarky remarks or sassy comments; he doesn't give off anything. I never thought I would see the day.

With them knowing everything, it would be dangerous for me to drag this out any longer. It has to happen soon and it will.

I walked over to the roll door and raised it to the top. It snapped in place. The brightness from the sun causes me to wince. I turned to face them, the darkness in me returning. Grittiness seeping through my tone. "Remember what I said. Not a fucking word to anyone."

They jumped up from the bed and scurried out of the unit, yelling back in unison, "We promise!"

Chapter 38: Heather

I thought I was going to pass out. Had Cory not found mail from SafeStorage in his mailbox, we would have never found Cryptic. There was no way in a million and one years, we would have known Jason was alive, living in the bodies of other people.

After explaining everything, I realized, Cryptic isn't a bad guy, he's just scorned. Unlike my father, who kidnaps and kills the innocent for his gain, Jason only harms people who deserve it. I've been living under the same roof as the monster while hunting the hero.

The drive home was longer than I imagined it would be. I don't remember driving, being zoned out most of the time while my body was on autopilot. *Do I help Cryptic get to my dad? Do I warn Roman?*

I visualized a life without Roman. Everything would change for me. I would have to live on my own. Possibly, would have to get a proper job. My journalism career would never take off. I wouldn't have the time to dedicate to blogging. It's not like journaling has been successful, anyway. I wouldn't lose much by letting it go.

What about Rosie? Why was she on the list and not me? Not that I want to be. I know she's as innocent as I am.

I cruised into the driveway, still out of it. Rosie's car wasn't in the garage. Roman is still in the hospital. I get some time alone. I need it.

I drag myself into the house, up the stairs, and into my room. Removing my clothes, I head to the shower and turn it to boiling. I position my body under the water and sob uncontrollably. My hand lays across my chest and I slide down the shower wall portraying the most dramatic scene in every movie.

As the streams crashed down on me, I wished for molted lava to pour onto my skin instead of water. Lava provides a scorching, sticky alternative, sitting on my skin, burning through all three layers until it shatters my core.

I reach for the handle and turn the shower off, hauling myself out. I wrapped my hair in one towel and wrapped the other around my body. Once again, I stare at the reflection of the girl looking back at me through the vanity mirror. I don't recognize her.

My feet guide me to the closet, pulling down a black jogger set. The towel drops to the floor, and I get dressed, sliding into a pair of sneakers to complete the look. My computer chimes, I slam it shut, not wanting to be social right now. I know they're worried about me. I'm worried about myself too. Deciding to deal with drama later, I tuck the computer under my armpit, gather my keys, and find my way mindlessly toward my car.

Approaching the Range Rover, I notice a photo on the windshield. It's snapped in place by the wipers. My hand reaches out to grab it and once in my possession, I realize it's a photo of Rosie. The same photo from the corkboard in Cryptic's unit.

I fiddle with the photo in my hand, investigating its contents.

Flipping the photo around, there is a written message displayed on the back. In chicken scratch it read:

To Heath, you didn't ask about her. Rosie is next on my list. Before I take her, I'll give you a chance to see her again.

Cryptic.

I rip the photo to pieces and let out a long, dreadful yelp. Stomping to my car door, it swings open, fury ripping through me. I slam my computer down into the passenger seat and start the ignition. Not giving the engine time to warm up, I throw the gear shifter in reverse and mash the gas, taking out the trashcan behind me.

The truck rocks back and forth from the force, causing my head to thrust forward immediately after it crashes into the headrest behind me. I seethe but ignore the pain, snatching the gear from reverse and moving it into drive.

The drive to the hospital was deadly. I ran every stoplight and stop sign. I weaved between vehicles that stood in the way. Without a care in the world, I was ready for death, if she was ready to take me.

On two wheels, my truck speeds up into the parking lot, then screeching to a halt, double parking while taking up two parking spots. The door slams as I exit the truck, turning to assess the damage from my fight with the trashcan.

I'm reunited with Roman again once arriving in his hospital room. He notices my disarray, the same visual Rosie gave him when she burst through this same hospital door. I crash into the seat next to his bed.

He croaks, "Everything okay?"

I retort, "Nothing is okay and it never will be."

I picked up the phone to dial Rosie. It rings but eventually sends me to voicemail. *He has her.*

Chapter 39: Jason

Rosie is in the passenger seat of my Tahoe as I drive us to the coffee shop. She's relaxed, knowing I'll take care of tonight's shipment. This will be the first and last favor I ever do for her.

"You remember the plan? All shipments are the same. The boat comes over full of containers. The crane will lift the containers and place them in the port's yard." She explains as if I haven't done my homework. As if she hasn't explained this same weak-ass plan over and over since the night I decided to help. "My dad's boss has already passed down the numbers of the containers that have our merchandise. Line up the men at every entrance and exit point. Appoint a few men to receive the containers."

She shifts her gaze to look out of the window. "Ian used to pop the locks on the containers we needed. I guess you will have to use another one of our men to do that for us." Her voice cracks. She misses him. "You will need to remove the locks and position the unmarked vans at different locations around the port. In the event of one van being compromised, make sure the vans depart at different times. Make sure every man is armed. If anyone strays from the plan, you shoot them. The drivers know the address of our drop location. They know to arrive at separate times and to take separate routes to get there."

I grip the steering wheel tighter. "I've already handled that part. You know I have this under control, Rosie. You may want to remember who you're talking to."

I park behind the coffee shop, allowing her time to finish her lesson on how to traffic humans. "I know. My dad is depending on me, and I want to make him proud." Proud isn't the word I would use for taking over an illegal family business. I'll let her believe whatever her deluded mind is telling her to believe.

The passenger door opens, and she turns to me before getting out. "Who knows, maybe one day we can run this business together."

"Rosie, get the hell out of my car and wait here until I return." I roll my eyes and the door slams. Rosie's figure walks up to the shop, unlocks the door, and disappears inside.

* * *

Upon first glance at the cabin, it looks vacant. A two-story wooden fixture that sits on a lake. Perfectly manicured lawn with no vehicles or tire marks visible.

I park the Tahoe at the back of the cabin, leaving behind my arsenal bag. Once inside, the men gather around a family-style table. An assortment of paper scattered in front of them. The chatters come to a halt and all turn to stare at me. Clouds of smoke blanket the air from the continuous chain puffing.

One with a cigarette still tipping his lips asks, "Christophe, what's up, man? We thought you were still at the hospital with Roman."

My feet shift, guiding me closer toward the men. "Rosie couldn't make it," I lie.

"Yeah, we don't take lightly to taking orders from a woman," he scoffs. He looks around the table to see if other men agree.

"That woman is going to be your boss if or when anything happens to Roman." I counter. "Let's discuss tonight's shipment so I can get this over with."

I breeze over the details of the plan, ensuring that I stationed men at every entrance and exit point. There were a few men assigned to each container. I appointed Larry, Ian's dad, who was seated at the table, to pop the locks on specific containers before the rest of the crew arrived.

Once the locks are popped, our men will move in, extract the merchandise from each container, and lead them to vans supplied by the organization. Drivers, already familiar with the drop location, are aware of their separate routes and arrival times. The plan was smooth and would be hard to fuck up.

The men rose from their seats, loading up on guns, screwing on silencers. I remind them of our meeting time, 1900. This means Larry will have the locks popped by 1830. That will give our men plenty of time to close in, but not too much time that would allow the merchandise to get any bright ideas.

The first part was over. Getting the men on board was easy. Now for part two. Where I conduct another meeting chewing over different details for the same shipment.

Chapter 40: Jason

I station the Tahoe in an alley that sits a few blocks away from the port. It's almost show time, but I arrived an hour early to prepare. I rarely get nervous, but to be completely honest, I can feel a few flutters low in my stomach.

A bulletproof vest wraps around my torso. The vest has velcro pockets positioned symmetrically in various areas, which give me ample space to store at least six knives. I sank razor-sharp knives into each hole, pulling a hooded jacket over my head to cover. I placed epinephrine syringes in my pants pocket. Silently apologized to my daughter, who I knew would not be proud of me right now.

I closed the door on the trunk and jogged through the darkness until reaching the port. A security guard is standing in the booth, unaware of my presence because he's nose-deep in his phone. I crouch out of sight while slipping my first knife out of a pocket on my vest. He smiles at something on his screen and my face fuses into a similar form because I know he will probably be the easiest kill I make tonight.

Still crouching, I creep over to the booth, slowly sliding the door open when I make it. The knife hiding behind my back in one hand while the other remains on the door. I say in a low grumble, "Roman's man." That worked the first time I came to do a job. Why not try it again?

His eyes widen at my presence, then dim once he realizes he has the authority, or so he thinks. He says, "You don't have permission to be here."

I slide the knife out from behind my back and quickly close the space between us, applying pressure over the guard's mouth and forcing him into the wall of the booth. His eyes nearly pop out of the sockets, and as much as I would love to see that, I don't have time to torment him. I flick the lights out by the switch on the wall behind the guard's head and everything goes dark. He's scared as shit, trembling beneath me so hard, I can feel his shakes quake through my body.

He whimpers something behind my hand, but I can't make out the garble, nor do I give a damn about what he's trying to say. With a firm grip on the knife, I sank it deep into his stomach. A loud groan rumbles behind my hand and I remove the knife, only to sink it in again. His body became heavy, leaning against mine as he went limp. I pushed him to the floor, where he landed on his side, blood pooling into a puddle beneath him. His body releases its last breath of air as I say, "I do now." I turned to leave the booth.

By now, Larry should be here popping locks. There are two containers on the list and they sit on opposite sides of the port. I can visually remember the numbers of the containers from the paper Rosie wrote them down on. If he comes from the direction I told him to, parking at Fish and Chips and walking over, he would go after the container that is second on the list first.

I made my way in that direction, leaning against random containers for cover. My heart is racing, knowing this plan can't fail. If I die here tonight, I won't make it to Roman. I won't live to see the day he dies.

The sound of metal clings, and I know I'm close. I peek around the container to see Larry with a crowbar positioned on the lock. My hand still grips the knife that was used to kill the guard, his blood painting the blade. I walk swiftly over to Larry, but still keeping quiet. He realizes my presence and maintains his hands in position. One hand slowly moves away from the handle of the crowbar and circles around his back.

In a soft tone, I say, "It's just me. Keep working." Hoping my arrival doesn't throw him off. After a brief pause, he stops attempting to grab for his gun and the clinging starts again, which lets me know he's accepting of my company.

He says, "Man, you scared me. I didn't know who you were." He lets out a light chuckle of relief.

Once within arm's reach, I snatch the gun from his backside and stab him in the side of his neck with my knife. Retracting the knife, blood spits out and a few drops land on my face. I lick at the drops that were on my lips and place his gun in my waistband, with the handle resting on my lower back.

His hand goes up to apply pressure to the wound and the crowbar falls to his side, his hands still gripping the handle. I grab the bar before it falls to the floor so it wouldn't create unnecessary noise. I leaned it up against the doors of the container.

Larry's body crashes on the ground. He's in a fetal position, using both hands to patch the wound on his neck. He coughs on his blood as it chokes him, filling his airway and restricting oxygen from entering.

I sat down, resting my back against the door. I listened to Larry die a slow death, drowning in his essence. More men should show shortly. All I have to do is wait.

The water sparkles thanks to the low light radiating from the moon. The sound of waves crashing against the dock provides me with a slight state of relaxation. My body is still uneasy at the thought of how many women and children were in captivity behind me. I refuse to look. Roman's advice proved to be slightly helpful: *never look at the merchandise.*

The headlights from approaching buses caught my attention. I stood from my seated position and focused on the shiny lights turning into the port. So the fun begins.

Chapter 41: Jason

I jog through the darkness to the opposite side of the port, leaving Larry's dead body behind. Every entry and exit should already have men stationed. My eyes dart around, constantly checking my surroundings. The only noise provided is the sound of waves crashing. Therefore, my silence is imperative.

A dark figure stands at attention before me, his back turned to me. He's a tall man, one from the cabin who I remember having a cigarette between his lips while talking. He's an arrogant prick, from what I can recall.

My pace slows, and the saliva in my mouth thickens. I still have my hand wrapped around the knife that already has two bodies on it. I'm about to add on a third. My position shifted to line up directly behind his figure. I hold the knife in the air like a dart, aiming at his backside.

My arms draw back like many times before and with full force, the knife shoots out of my grasp like a bullet. The blade connects, embedding itself into his skull. I could hear a thud on impact. After a split second, his body falls forward, landing face-first against the concrete, shattering his facial structure.

With adrenaline surging, my next target should be a few yards away. My feet dance to their own beat, remembering the mapping of this place from when I visited as Ian. The next target was in sight. He's standing at attention just like the last.

I circle my hand around my back and feel the coldness of Larry's gun in the palm of my hand. Silencer still intact, I aim at the side profile of this guy's head, ready to pull the trigger. Fire erupts from the tip of the gun from the combustion of the bullet leaving the chamber. The bullet enters one side of his skull, spraying blood from the wound, and leaves his skull on the opposite end. His body follows the direction of the bullet, landing on his side. He dies immediately.

The process is the same each time I encounter one of Roman's men, taking them out one by one. A bullet provides quick and quiet deaths to avoid alerting the others. With eight bodies down, there are only a few more lives to take before I can pop the locks on each can and inspect the merchandise without interruption.

I assigned two men to each can whose jobs are to lead the women out of the container, to their perspective vans. They don't know those vans aren't coming. I sent them to a different location.

I spot them approaching the container that was first on the list. The only problem is, if they make it to the can and realize someone hasn't popped the lock, they'll grow suspicious. I can't have that.

They're mingling like they've done this job too many times, and it's a normal sunny Saturday morning. Almost like they're taking a long stroll along the beach, making small-talk and giggling like a bunch of high school girls.

Their chatter provided a higher volume of noise, overpowering the waves crashing, and giving me the opportunity to get creative. In a full sprint, gun in hand, I run up behind the men, aiming for the man's head on the right.

I pull the trigger while still sprinting, and it clicks. *Damnit. This is why I don't use guns. Never know when this fucking thing goes out of bullets.* The men startle, stopping their conversation and halting in their tracks. Without a new clip to reload and with no time to spare, I think quickly while still sprinting toward them.

With the gun raised above my head, once I'm close enough, I swing the metal into the back of the head of the first guy. Providing him with a successful pistol whip, knocking him down unconscious. I try the same method with the second guy but he grabs my raised hand, holding it in midair before I can send the metal down crashing into his skull.

His hand circles his back, while my free hand slips a knife free from my vest. While he's whipping his gun around to the front, the heaviness of the metal slows him down and I have a brief second to slice a deep laceration into the arm that's holding the gun. He lets go of my arm as a reflex, thanks to the pain surging from the wound.

I circle behind him, dragging the knife across his throat. While I have him pinned against my torso, I continue cutting into his neck with the knife, aligning my arm with his. My fingers encase each of his fingers, our arms melting into one as I guide the gun to aim at the friend he was frolicking with. My index finger slides over his and I squeeze, applying pressure to his finger and, in turn, applying pressure to the trigger.

A bullet releases and implants into the skull of his friend. Our arms move in sync while I aim at the head of the guy in my grasp. The knife still slicing into his throat with my left hand, and my index finger remains overlapping his finger, guiding him with my right hand. I squeeze the trigger once again, and fire bursts from the tip of the silencer. I can smell the gun smoke after the bullet releases.

Crimson and brain matter squirt out while the bullet travels through his brain and exits out the other side of his jaw. His jaw bones cracked while the bullet impaled. His body went limp in my arm, dropping his head into the bend and putting him in a headlock. The weight of his body became heavy. I gaped both arms open and his body released from my hold, sending him crashing to the ground.

With not much time to spare, I raced to the other can. Sweat dribbled down my hairline, passing my temples, as I sprinted. Frustrated voices can be heard in the distance, but the volume increases as I draw closer.

"Why the fuck didn't Larry cut the lock?" One man asked.

The other man pacing, gun in hand. He says, "I don't know Sergey, but something is off."

Sergey bangs on the lock while the other guy paces. They're both fuming.

I approach the men unarmed, or so they think, with both hands visible. I yell over to them once in the open, "Men?" They both turn to look at me. Sergey, the man who was venting his anger on the lock, turns and looks at me as if he has been caught stealing a piece of candy. The other man, who was pacing, raised his gun to me, finger clearly on the trigger, prepared to shoot.

"Hey man, slow your roll. It's just me." I say with a bold smile on my face, hoodie still hiding most of my features.

They settle a little from the sound of my voice, but not enough, which tells me they know something is off.

Gun still pointed at me, the man said, "What are you doing here? I thought you were watching over to make sure this goes as planned. Something didn't feel right when I noticed the lock, but you being here now lets me know something is wrong."

Fuck it. I quickly reach my hands under the hoodie and pull two knives out of my vest. Someone notices my attempts and I hear the sweet, silent sound of a bullet leaving the chamber and coursing through the silencer.

The weight of a dumpster lunges into my chest and pushes me backward. I fall to the ground face-up and can hear the men speaking violently in Russian a few feet away from me. The pain rips through me like a current. The pressure from the bullet lies on my body like a blanket, rendering me paralyzed.

Heavy footsteps approach while I gaze up at the stars, not blinking. The heads of both men come into peripheral view. They stand over me for a few seconds to talk, deciding what they're going to do. It's not a straightforward choice to kill me, being that I'm Roman's right hand. I was about to charge them with two knives. They had every right to be conflicted.

I tighten my grasp on the handles with both hands and shoot my arms up like I'm making a snow angel, slicing the blade through their ankles. I hasten to get out of the direction of the impending gunfire. Bullets fly in multiple directions as they squeeze their triggers while also falling to the ground in agony.

I roll behind Sergey's broad body, using it as a shield, his trigger-happy friend sinking bullets into him. His body slowed down the bullets enough that the pressure from their impact was minor when they reached my vest. I pull a gun out of Sergey's waistband and fire in the direction the oncoming bullets are coming from, still hiding completely behind Sergey's dead body.

I hear a yelp and know I've hit the other guy. So I fire some more until I can no longer hear any sounds of life escape from him. I peek my head up from behind Sergey and notice the friend is dead, too.

Getting up from my previous position, my body sore, I raise the hoodie to assess the damage. A few bullets sunk tip-deep into my vest, but not enough to contact my skin.

I drag my weak body to the container where I killed Larry, the crowbar still lying beside it. Taking the same steps I took when I did this job as Ian, the lock cracks under pressure from the crowbar and falls to the ground. Crowbar in tow, I retreat to the opposite side of the port and do the same with the second can.

Pulling out my burner phone, I called the one contact in the contact list. No one speaks. I say, "They're ready." With no acknowledgment, I ended the call and waited.

A few moments later, a bus pulls in, backing up close to the container. When the air brakes release, clouds of dirt puff off the ground. The double doors swing open and Lisa exits the bus. She asked, "You did it?"

I grumble while holding my chest, "It's done."

Chapter 42: Heather

I've never driven a bus before, but I knew what needed to be done. When Lisa reached out to me and told me about Jason's plan, I had no doubts that saving these women from Roman was the only option.

Lisa and Jason spoke for a moment before he took off to help Cory, who drove the other bus, load up the women and children from the other container. Lisa and I will unload this one.

I stepped off the bus and joined Lisa. She looked at me with eyes full of wonder. "Are you ready?" She asked.

I know she's expecting me to leave her stranded. She doesn't think I can handle it. I need to see what my dad has been doing all these years. Seeing makes it real to me.

I answer, "I'm ready." My bottom lip trembles as the lie leaves my lips. We walk over to the container.

Lisa grabs the handle, twisting it outward, and pulling the lever, opening the box. She fumbles with the flashlight while whimpers erupt from inside the can. My heart breaks when she finally switches the flashlight on.

Women and children with dirt smudged into their skin look at us in fear. I can't imagine how long they've been sitting in here, packed like sardines. The smell was atrocious from urine, stool, and vomit.

My stomach churns, but not from the smell or the visual. I'm disgusted by the thought of my dad running this organization. Being proud of something so inhumane rocks me to my core. I want to rid myself of everything he's ever given me. I want the memories of him wiped from my recollections. I want to cleanse myself of him completely, even wiping his legacy in the community away like he never existed.

"Oh, my," Lisa gasps as she stares into the sea of eyes. We share the same glance at each other. Both with disbelief and disappointment.

Lisa says with a cracked voice, "We are here to help. We want to take you all somewhere safe. I'll help you to the bus while she," Lisa points to me, "helps you out of this filthy container."

The whimpers turned into cries of relief; the volume amplified because of the enclosure. I began guiding the women and children out. They filed in a line, following Lisa's lead to the bus. Some were reluctant to come, which is understandable, but I reassured them of their safety using a low, sweet tone and a soft voice. I can only imagine how those poor women and children were responding to Cory and Jason.

With the bus fully packed beyond maximum capacity, some sitting in the aisle, I was ready to get them somewhere more comfortable. Lisa says her goodbyes to them while her hand lies on my shoulder for support.

We are both weak from exhaustion, not physically, but mentally. No one should ever go through this or see people treated this way. What gives someone the right to think they could own or sell another person? Even worse, what gives them the right to think they could kill and trade the organs of a person? The amount of trauma these victims are going to live with is enough to make the rest of their lives miserable.

She turns to me and says, "Take them to the women's shelter. I'm going to meet Jason. When you and Cory finish, you know where we will be." Before turning to leave, she adds, "Make sure all of them make it inside and get out of there before the cops show. We don't want them asking questions before what happens next."

She winks at me. I'm fully aware of what is coming. I'm just not ready for it and I don't think I ever will be.

Chapter 43: Jason

Lisa helped me to the Tahoe, where a change of clothes awaited me. This was going to be the last time I stepped foot in Tom Ford loafers. I never want to even see these fucking shoes again. I dressed in a suit and slipped into the passenger seat while Lisa drove us to the hospital.

We sat in the truck until the sun rose. I used that time to sleep, needing the energy for tonight. Roman was to be discharged today, and I wanted to be the first to welcome him home. Lisa and I grabbed a coffee from the cafeteria while the nurse prepared Roman for his departure. We sat at the table, sipping our warm drinks, when breaking news interrupted the scheduled program.

A video from a bird's-eye view of the port is playing on the television screens. My lips tear from the mouth of my coffee cup as my head turns to one television in the cafeteria. The view changes and a reporter speaks into the camera, her face becoming too familiar with all the chaos I've been causing.

She stares at the camera with her hand placed on the piece in her ear for a moment before speaking. "We are at the Port of Claireville with sad news. Behind me are containers that house the essentials used to maintain this community. However, we have found that some of these cans do not contain material.

Unfortunately, people were being held captive in two of them. Last night, someone brought two busloads of women and children to the women's shelter. All of them had the same story and were kidnapped."

She clears her throat and continues, "The Claireville's Police Department was dispatched to investigate the port. When they arrived, police officers found a guard stabbed to death in the guard booth." Regret is buried deep in my lower stomach hearing the reporter speak of the guard. I broke a promise by killing the innocent, even if he was collateral damage. "In different areas of the yard, they discovered many other male bodies, all armed. Some had bullet wounds. They found some individuals with stab wounds. They have not been identified yet. The containers contained feces and bodily fluids, suggesting that our victims had been inside them for a while. We extend our heartfelt condolences to the families of all victims who were found, whether they were rescued or deceased. This is an open investigation. If anyone has information, please call the number in the banner below." A 1-800 number scrolls at the bottom of the screen.

She says, "Thanks for choosing Channel 3 News."

I resumed sipping my coffee and hoped like hell the television in Roman's room wasn't on.

Chapter 44: Jason

I grab the handle on the door of Roman's room, preparing to enter. Either he's going to be furious, wondering how his men died and who allowed his merchandise to run away. Or he's going to be relieved knowing he could finally leave this place.

The door swings open with no help on my behalf. The nurse standing on the other side of the threshold yelps. Out of breath, she says, "Oh good. You're here. He's ready," she speaks with one hand holding her chest. She goes for a wheelchair while we walk into the room, taking in the environment.

Roman is sitting erect in the bed, a smile creeping across his face, then slowly fades when he notices Lisa. He asks, "Who is the lady?"

I answer, "No one." Because it's not his business who she is, and that should be the least of his concerns.

The patient bag on the floor rings, vibrating and shifting across the tile. I look at Roman, but his eyes dart in a different direction, ignoring whoever is calling. He says, "It's been ringing nonstop all day, but I don't have the energy to talk. I want to rest. My body is still weak, and so is my mind."

I truly don't give a shit, but I give him a sympathetic smile because that's what his friend, Christophe, would have done.

The phone rings again right before his nurse returns with

the wheelchair. I allow her to help him out of the bed and into the chair. I push Roman out of the hospital, letting Lisa take the bag so Roman doesn't change his mind about the phone thing.

We help Roman to the truck and leave the parking lot, heading for the coffee shop. While en route, Roman asks, "Where are we going? My home isn't in this direction."

I counter, "We are going to your home away from home. You remember the coffee shop where you spend most of your time?"

"Yea, but I told you I wanted to relax. I can't relax there." His voice is harsh, I pay it no mind. Soon, I'll shut him up permanently.

"At least let me stop to get a caramel macchiato," I tease. He doesn't respond.

I park around the back of the shop and kill the engine. I turn to Lisa and say, "Give me a second. I'll be right back."

She responds, "I know, but hurry. I don't want to sit in the truck with this asshole for much longer than I have to." She casts a dark look over at Roman. His eyes widen as the vein visibly throbs in his forehead from the disrespect. His jaw stiffens, but he keeps his mouth shut.

"I won't be long," I say.

I disappear into the inside of the shop, taking the stairs that lead up to a small studio space where I know Rosie awaits me. By now, I know she has seen the news and gotten the details of last night. I prepare for the ambush.

Opening the door, I realize I didn't prepare enough. Rosie catches my presence and foams at the mouth, baring her teeth as she stomps over to me. With balled fists, she started banging on my chest, hurling blow after blow into me as hard as she could. I grabbed her arms after being tired of her treating me like a punching bag before her men moved in on me.

"Take your hands off of her." One says from behind me.

Turning around to get a good visual of the bodyguard, I notice Heather and Cory are in the corner, staying out of the way. Their guilt is obvious. Maybe Rosie doesn't know the part they played yet.

I muse, "Or what big guy? You're going to kill me?"

He tilts his head and says, "I don't mind, but I won't do it unless she tells me to." He raises his chin in Rosie's direction, who is now being shielded by a second guard.

"If you must," I say, while slowly backing away. I reach behind my back for a knife and the guard pulls out his.

The blade flickers in the light as he smiles, showcasing one gold tooth. We circle each other, silently deciding which of us will make the first move. I charge for him on a fake, and he swings the blade in my direction. He misses. I shove the blade into the side of his abdomen.

A loud roar rips out of him, causing Heather and Rosie to scream in fear. Bodyguard number two charges, a switchblade in his hand. I'm prepared for him, ready to take them both on. I remove another knife from my vest. He makes the first move, jaw ready to snap as he stomps in my direction. His eyes are soulless.

I fiddle with the knife, interchanging it between my fingers. Aiming for his head, my arm drew back and snapped forward, sending the knife soaring through the air. He shifts to the side, and the knife tip pierces his ear. It sticks a landing into the wall a fingernail width away from Rosie's head.

She screams a deathly scream while eyeing the blade next to her. Her body flushes against the wall like she's pinned by the knife. The guard snapped his head in her direction, fury ignited in his demeanor. He turns to me and growls, ready to bulldoze me. He runs full speed, or as fast as his gigantic frame would allow. I time his steps, counting down until when he makes it to me.

When he's seconds away, I drop to my knees and slide around the floor, rounding his enormous body, and slicing into his calf deeply. Blood drains down to his ankle while his frame continues until he lands inside the wall, creating a massive hole in the structure. He dips forward, his torso stuck in between the wall's frame. The sound of boards cracking beneath him.

Amongst the chaos, the guard lying beside me found the opportunity to sink his blade into my leg. I yell in agony, the feeling of warm blood soaking through my pants. I grit, tightening my jaw hard to cause enough discomfort, keeping my mind away from what I'm about to do. I circle my hand around the handle and snatch the knife out of my leg, simultaneously turning around to sink my blood-soaked tip into the eyeball of this asshole.

Cory vomits in the corner, while Heather consoles him. I have no time to think or apologize. I remove the knife, and his eyeball comes with it. The optic nerve dangles at the end, dribbling blood onto the floor. I sink the knife into him repeatedly, and with every stab, his eye squishes, oozing clear fluid.

This time, Heather vomits, watching me continue to stab a knife into his dead body. The guard, who has become one with the wall, groans, still in pain. I stand on a limp, holding my wound, and walked over to the only guard that was alive.

The knife sank into his back, eyeball matter mixing with his blood as his legs became paralyzed because of the piercing of his spine. Tilting his head back, because I am growing tired of this circus, I saw the knife back and forth into his neck, attempting to sever his entire fucking head off.

I could hear jumbled words in the distance. Deep in thought and rage, I can't focus on anything around me. I continue to seesaw the knife through fat and muscle, getting down to the bone. His bones dull my knife, causing me to become angrier.

The voices in the distance grow louder when I come to. It's Cory, he's screaming for me to stop.

"Stop. Please stop," he pleads.

When I turn in his direction, he tenses because a rabid look is etched in my expression. The worried look on his face, with tears streaming down, brought me to reality. I've never seen Cory scared, worried, or anything other than being a hard ass with a smart mouth. I drop the guard's head. It bobs into the hole space until it eventually stills.

Stepping away, I look over at Rosie, wincing. Ignoring her, I pull out my burner and call Lisa.

"Bring him in. Bring my bag," I demand.

While waiting for Lisa, I tear my shirt. Wrapping it around my leg above the knife wound. The shirt applied pressure to my vessels, halting the bleeding.

A few moments pass, and a knock sounds from the door. I open it for Lisa, who throws a black bag at my feet and rolls Roman into the room. Roman grips the armrests tightly but says nothing.

He thrashes side to side in his seat like a child having a tantrum. Double-stranded rope is securing his arms, legs, and torso, preventing him from doing much. Duct tape keeps his lips together. I punch him in his temple, knocking him unconscious.

Rosie screams, "What did you do to him?"

I limp over to her, eyes dark, brows furrowed. I don't answer her. Instead, I silently reached next to her head, pulling the knife out of the wall. She lets out a relieved sigh when I turn to leave her immediate space. Lisa passed me, closing the space, ropes in hand. She ties Rosie up, wrapping her arms at the wrists and legs at the ankles.

Heather asks, "Lisa, what the fuck are you doing?"

Lisa doesn't answer.

The sounds of Rosie's cries fall on deaf ears.

Chapter 45: Heather

I've never seen Cory this quiet. He always has something to say. Even if it's just words of encouragement for me to stay positive through this entire process. He has uttered nothing since we left the shelter.

This morning, during the news report, he cracked a grin, watching as the news covered last night's ordeal. After Jason's arrival, he's been shaking uncontrollably in the corner. My attempts to calm him haven't been successful, the knife fight only making the situation worse.

Rosie being tied up put me in the same state as Cory, wondering if I would be bound next. It hasn't happened yet. Jason positioned Roman next to Rosie, facing Cory and me. Jason has been limping since being wounded in the leg by one of the guard's knives, but that didn't slow him down. He mustered up enough energy to drag the body to the wall where the other guard remained flapped over, leaning into the hole in the wall bent at his hip.

Lisa returned with two-gallon jugs of what smelled like gasoline. She dropped them on the floor of the flat, and my fight-or-flight instincts kicked in. Jason eyed me as I attempted to creep to the exit, Cory in tow.

"If you leave, I'll have to kill you," he says, jaw tense. Lisa shoots a look over to me, signaling that he's serious and I should listen. We resumed our places in the corner.

Jason rips a knife out of the guard's stomach and positions it on the tape that's keeping Roman's mouth shut. Roman grunts behind the tape, his words inaudible.

Jason warns, "If you scream or don't do as I say, I'll end you." He pats his index finger along the tape, measuring where Roman's mouth parts, and glides the bloody knife across, giving Roman a hole to speak through. Roman remains quiet.

Rosie babbles, "What do you plan to do with us? What do you want?"

Jason responds, "Funny you ask. Tell your sister what you've been up to."

Her eyes widen as she quiets, refusing to speak. Jason aggressively limps over to her, knife still planted in his palm. He aims the tip at her face and growls, "Tell her," he demands.

Rosie takes in her environment. Roman is bound to a wheelchair, his guards dead on the other side of the room, and a crazy man holding a knife to her face. She has no choice other than to do as she's told. The realization causes words to spill from her mouth.

Rosie explains, "Dad doesn't have any sons. He had to choose between you and me to take over the business. He chose me."

I question, "Which business are we referring to?" I knew the answer to that question, but I wanted to be sure.

"Well, my naïve, self-centered sister, I'm sure as hell not talking about the coffee shop."

Jason slashes the knife across her face, blood bubbles from the cut and trickles down her cheek. Roman seethes, "Don't you fucking touch her again."

Jason's head snaps in his direction, "Or what Roman? Don't

answer that. You'll be dead soon, anyway."

Rosie's tears mixed with the blood draining from her wound. She begins, "I-, I started preparing to take over our family business, the trafficking business, about a year ago." She stutters. My legs weaken. "I've been working alongside dad to understand the ins and outs of the business. I'll be able to run it when he steps down."

I ask, "Why didn't you tell me?" Tears surge from my eyes as well.

"Because I didn't know how." She wipes at her face while Jason limps across the room, his crippled form of pacing.

Jason says, "Now, Roman, it's your turn. Tell me about what happened in this same location five years ago?"

Roman reddens, eyes darting between Rosie and me. "Christophe, why the fuck do you care about what happened? You know what you did."

Jason says, "That's not what I asked you. I want you to tell your girls what happened. I want them to hear it from you."

His fingers circle the armrests on the wheelchair, gripping them tight, turning his knuckles from a shade of pink to an ashy white.

Jason adds, "Start from the beginning."

Roman explained, "This location is a prime area for a coffee shop, as you can see." He looks around the flat. "I was determined to build my shop here. Before the shop, someone built a house here and the owner, who was a piece of shit, refused to move." Jason's head snaps in Roman's direction. Roman notices and chooses his next words wisely.

He continues, "I asked repeatedly if he would move, letting me have this location. I even offered him a large amount of money he couldn't refuse. He refused it anyway. After multiple attempts to get him to leave, I sent you over to burn the place down." He casts a look at Christophe. He doesn't know that's not Christophe standing before him, but I'm sure he's going to find those details out pretty soon.

Roman's phone rang, and all of our attention diverted to his phone until the ringing stopped.

Jason demands, "Continue."

Roman explains, "I sent Christophe to burn the house down because it was my only option. I thought only Jason would be in the home." His voice quiets, "I didn't know his daughter would be here too. She was supposed to be at camp."

Jason growls deeply, controlling his urges. Cory's hand finds mine again and grips it tightly.

Jason asks, "So you built the coffee shop on top of my daughter's last resting place?" Confusion engulfed Roman's face. "Answer me," Jason demands.

"Yes, I built the shop anyway. I needed everything to be perfect. If the coffee shop made enough money, I could launder most of the money I made from organ trafficking through here. Trafficking is a very lucrative business, and there's a lot of money to be made. But the illegal money I process through the coffee business has to be replaced with legal money. I needed a good turnout for washing to be successful. That is why the location was important." He explained in a matter-of-fact tone.

Jason asked, "What about the family that lived here?"

Roman answered, "Eventually, I overcame their deaths once I got what I wanted. Their deaths were collateral for a greater cause."

Jason raced over to my dad, fuming. He buried the knife deep in Roman's leg, twisting the knife from side to side. Roman screeches but Jason slaps a palm over Roman's mouth and continues to dig with the knife, sinking it deeper.

Cory yelps, "Jason, stop. That's enough."

Jason obliges and limps away from Roman without breaking eye contact.

Rosie spits, "Christophe, why the fuck do you care? You burned it down."

I answered before Jason could, "That's because he's not Christophe."

Roman questions, "What the fuck are you talking about, Heather?"

Jason rests his back against the wall, not in a hurry to admit the truth. He pulls out a box of cigarettes and lights one. My eyes dart between the cherry red tip and the jugs of gasoline.

I spoke, "Jason didn't die here five years ago. He escaped." Roman relaxes, thinking my comment is bullshit. I continue, "That night, Hank died as well. After being revived, Jason regained consciousness while in Hank's body. Jason has been living as Hank until recently."

Roman laughs, laughter mixed with amusement and agony from his leg wound.

I ignore him and continue, "Jason has killed and embodied Melissa, Ian, and now, Christophe." Rosie gasps and Roman continues to find humor in my explanations. "Everyone he has killed, he slits their throats. Look at Christophe's throat. There is a long, jagged scar resting on his neck. That is from the night he embodied Christophe." My focus turns to Roman. "Remember that night of the dinner party? I'm sure that's when Christophe started acting weird after hanging Ian, didn't he?" Roman stops laughing and straightens in his chair. "That's not Christophe standing before you, Roman. That is Jason, the man you killed."

Roman eyes Jason, trying to reason with himself how something nearly impossible could be true. Roman's phone rings again, interrupting the silence. Again, we wait until the ringing stops.

Jason chimes in, "You don't have to believe her, Roman. You'll die here tonight regardless of what you believe. You'll suffer the same fate you gave my daughter, Elizabeth, and the fate you tried to give me." He took another long drag and flipped the lit cigarette in Roman's lap.

The tip burned through Roman's pants, breaking the barrier between the lit tip and Roman's skin. He shakes, thrusting his hips to toss the cigarette away from his lap, but it doesn't work. He wails. The wailing stops after Roman pisses himself. His urine putting out the burn.

Jason releases a disturbed laugh. Roman's face flushes.

"You got what you wanted. You built the coffee shop and groomed your daughter to run the trafficking business. Damn, you must feel like the father of the year." Jason ponders.

"I had no choice," Roman admits, looking down at the burn hole in his lap.

Jason hisses, "You always have a choice."

Roman repeats, "I had no choice." The room falls quiet. Roman raises his head and looks at me. "Grab my phone out of the hospital bag, Heather. Next time it rings, answer it. That is who runs the show. That is my boss calling. She decides. All this time, you thought it was me. As I told you in the hospital, I'm just a puppet." He points at the phone. "But she owns the entire international organization of the organ trade. She is who you want, not me." He turns to Rosie, "Rosie, you're going to want to hear this too."

Jason stills, "Don't give me some bullshit story. That will not get you out of this. Remember, you still ordered for my home to be burned down."

Roman says, "Just answer the phone next time it rings. She will call again soon. She won't stop until she reaches me."

I peeled Cory's fingers away from my hand and bent down to rummage through Roman's hospital bag. My heart raced while the phone rested in my hand. I don't want to speak to the owner of the entire organ trade. What am I supposed to say?

Everyone stared at the phone, waiting for it to ring. Everyone other than Jason, who had the jugs in his grasp. He tipped them over, starting at the dead bodies. The aroma of gasoline filled my nostrils, burning them.

He soaked their bodies in fuel while pouring the combustible fluid along the edges of the walls, stopping a few feet away from the door on each side. He took his position against the wall again, keeping the knife in his hand.

The wait continued.

The phone rang, and my heart sank. The fierce beating felt in the pit of my stomach. Everyone turned to look at me. Rosie, still bound, started grinding her teeth. The word *Karen* crossed the screen with a green button for answer, and a red button for decline bounced underneath it.

My finger trembled over the answer button. My tongue was heavy in my mouth. I clicked answer and placed the phone on speaker. Shakes took over my body as I was on the verge of vomiting again.

The female voice on the other end said, "Roman?" She paused. Screaming into the phone, she continues, "Roman, you let my men die and merchandise get away? Who did this? You are an incompetent piece of shit. I can't believe I trusted you with a responsibility this big. I knew you wouldn't be capable of handling it. You fucking fool. The police will ask questions and that is on you for making me vulnerable because you couldn't follow simple fucking instructions. Now get my girls out of that shitty town and bring them home to me. Do you hear me, Roman? Bring my daughter's home."

Daughters? As in Rosie and me?

The line goes quiet, but I could still hear her breathing on the other line. Roman turns to Rosie and says, "Your attitude and fire have always reminded me of your mother." He turns to me and says, "You look just like her."

Chapter 46: Heather

Rosie squeaks, "Mom?"

Karen speaks, "Rosie? Is that you?"

I hit the red button to end the call. Things were weird enough. I couldn't handle them becoming any weirder. Rosie steams, "Heather, why would you do that?"

I seethe, "We don't know her, Rosie. All we know is she left us and that's it. I don't even remember what she looks like and I know you don't either. You were too young when she left."

Rosie goes quiet. Roman speaks, "Your mother left because she wanted me to follow in Dmitri's footsteps. Dmitri Yuri Volkov is your grandfather. I refused to leave you two. I didn't want to be the lord of trafficking. When your mother realized I was adamant about not taking over, she took over instead. She chose this life over raising you two."

My heart stopped, or so I thought it did. I hated them both.

Jason's back finally leaves the wall as he says, "Alright, I'm growing tired of this shit. Now, time for the encore."

He removes a lighter from his pocket and bends down to ignite the fire, starting with the bodies of the two dead guards. The flames blaze, engulfing the bodies in its wake. Cory and I shift away from the heat.

It follows the same path Jason made. Flames crawl up the

walls, licking the ceiling. Rosie and Roman yell. Jason walks over to Rosie, who is inching away from the wall, trying to get as far as she can from the heat.

Jason cuts the ties at her legs, but leaves her arms bound. She gets up to make a run for it and he grabs her by the throat. He says to Lisa, "Get the syringe out of my bag."

Lisa does as she's told. She slips a syringe with an orange cap out of his bag. Clear liquid already rests inside of it. I ask, "What are you going to do?"

Jason says in a low tone, "Out of everyone here, you are one of the few who knows what's about to happen." Lisa slips the syringe into Jason's pocket.

Jason wraps his arm around Rosie's forehead and tilts her head back, elongating her neck.

Roman wriggles in his seat. He begs, "Please don't do this."

Jason shrugs his shoulder. "She's just collateral damage." The knife drags across Rosie's throat, her scarlet flowing down her neck as she bares her teeth from the pain. He holds her up, forcing us to watch as Rosie bleeds out.

The fire continues, smoke filling the room. Roman thrusts back and forth, trying to propel the wheelchair forward as the fire grows near him. Rosie's body finally drops to the floor when Jason lets her go. He bends down to release the bondage around her arms and she encases her hands around her neck.

Roman screams, "Rosie!" He looks at Jason, "You bastard. You killed my daughter."

Jason's eyes darken. His face turns sinister. "You're next," he says. "I'm going to kill you with the blood of your daughter."

Jason slashes the garment off of Roman, his skin now visible. Taking the knife, he carves Roman's skin, crimson paints his body. Jason slashes every inch of Roman's skin, growling with every cut. He's enjoying this.

Watching my father die was something I prepared for. Watching Rosie die, I couldn't live with. I rush over to her and fall to my knees. "Rosie, stay with me." I cry. "Please stay with me." I could still hear my dad being sliced in the background. His groans were deeply disturbing. "Rosie, I'm begging you, please." I plead while her arms go limp at her side, the light from her eyes dimming.

I interlock my fingers and place them on her chest. I pound. "Stay with me, Rosie." This was my first time doing CPR. I remember a little from a class I took once a few years ago. I scream in agony, "Rosie!"

Jason turns around, finally noticing Rosie's demise. He raises a knife to his throat and, with the same twisted look on his face, he says, "Now, for my favorite part." His eyes trail further up past where I'm performing life-saving measures on Rosie to behind us, where Cory is standing.

Lisa screams, "Cory, what the fuck are you doing?"

I don't turn around to see what has their attention. I'm still focusing on Rosie. My arms burning, my heart racing, I continue to pound on my sister's chest. Praying she doesn't leave me.

Chapter 47: Jason

With the knife pressing against my throat, I look up at Cory, who is crying painful tears with both hands wrapped around his own blade. The tip aimed directly at his chest. What the hell is he doing?

Annoyance in my tone, I ask, "Cory, we don't have time for this shit. She's dying. This needs to happen now."

Cory cries, "Put it down. This is not your body to take."

I pressed the knife's tip into my throat, cutting a little flesh and causing it to bleed. Cory's eyes widen, and his grip on the knife tightens.

I ask, "If it's not my body to take, then whose is it?"

Cory hisses, "It's mine."

Lisa screams at him to put the blade down. Now, she's crying. What the fuck is going on? Lisa babbles, "Just tell him, Cory. Please. Tell him so we can end this."

I quiz, "Tell me what?" Do I really want to know? Cory has been a pain in my ass since I've met him. Of course, he would pull this shit when I'm close to revenge. I cough from the smoke filling my lungs. I watch as Heather's compressions weaken. She's getting tired.

Shouting, I ask again, "Tell me what?"

Cory shoves the knife into his chest while screaming like a

lunatic. Blood trickles from his mouth, pouring over his hands still wrapped around the handle. He gurgles on his blood while saying, "I-, I'm. Dad, I'm-."

Dad?

My eyes widen, and I drop the knife from my grasp. Sweat pouring from my temples, I drop to my knees beside Heather. I shove her out of the way while resuming compressions on Rosie.

Cory's body drops face forward on the floor. The pressure of his body causes the knife to bury deeper into his chest cavity. I've seen a lot of gruesome shit, but that was nasty, and dramatic.

Sweat drips from my face onto Rosie's body. I continue to compress. I yell to Lisa, "Lisa, get the syringe. Inject her now."

Lisa races over, popping the cap and stabbing epinephrine into Rosie's thigh. I take a break from compressions and deliver two breaths into Rosie's mouth. Without lag, I continue compressions.

After a few rounds, I check the pulse in Rosie's neck. It's thready, but it's there.

Lisa says, "Jason, we have to go. The fire is growing. This building will cave on us soon."

I simmer, "Lisa, my daughter's soul might be here. She's looking for a body and this is the only opportunity I have to save her. Don't get me started on the fact that you knew. This entire time, you knew."

Lisa cries, "I did. It was Elizabeth the entire time. I knew."

Tears cloud my vision as I look down at Rosie's body. Her eyes slowly open as I caress her head. *Please be in there, baby girl. Daddy's here.*

The heat from the fire burns my skin as Roman yells in the

background. The fire has made its way to him and he burns, just as I did. Rosie whispers, "Dad?"

"Is it you, Elizabeth?"

In a low tone, Elizabeth says, "Yes. It's me, dad. It's Elizabeth."

I howled a loud, painful cry while holding the only piece of me that was still alive, my child. My heart shattered into a million pieces, repaired itself, and shattered again. Every piece of me is now broken, now vulnerable. My body is weak from the amount of pain and energy I've expelled throughout this journey of vengeance.

I knew Cory was weird. A sassy, smart-mouthed boy didn't suit him. He got under my skin often because he reminded me of myself. I want to be in this moment forever, especially after thinking I would never have this opportunity again. It feels surreal, but I refuse to believe this is all a dream.

I replayed all the times Cory's sass annoyed me. All the moments I saw myself in him, it wasn't a coincidence, it was Elizabeth. When he explained astral projection, I chalked it up to research, never realizing it could have been an experience. I should have probed more and asked questions. I would have had her in my arms sooner.

I sobbed while rocking her back and forth in my arms while the flames continued to crackle and burn around us. The smoke made it difficult to breathe but I didn't care about breathing while I finally held my daughter. I would rather go up in smoke than let her go again. Lisa's screams of how we needed to leave were ignored. Roman's cries from being barbecued, were disregarded. The only voice to pull me to reality is Elizabeth's. She choked, "Dad, I can't breathe."

I scooped up Elizabeth's new body, her haunted eyes now beautiful to me. Unraveling the tourniquet from my leg, I wrapped the bloody shirt around my hand to create a barrier between my palm and the hot door handle.

I call back to Heather and Lisa, "Let's go." My attention turns to Elizabeth in my arms. I say to her, "I'm taking you home."

She buries her head in my chest as I reach for the door that the fire is blazing around. I limp with her in my arms down the steps. We left Roman's screams behind in the flat.

We head outside to where Heather's Ranger Rover is parked. I lightly place her in the back seat. Heather crawls into the driver's side and Lisa claims the passenger seat.

"I'll be right back," I promise Elizabeth.

Removing the lighter from my pocket, I crouch and spark it under the Tahoe. It can burn with the rest of them. The fire ignites and I jump into the backseat of Heather's truck. She starts the engine and throws the transmission into drive.

A relieved sigh leaves my lips as I turn my head over to Elizabeth. She's here. My baby girl is here with me. She catches my gaze and smiles.

Every ounce of pain I've felt and every person I've killed led up to this moment. I would do it all again if that meant I would be reunited with my daughter. I can only pray for anyone who tries to take her away from me again.

Chapter 48: Heather

I lost Roman and Rosie tonight. Karen, my mother, is alive and is running the trafficking organization I thought Roman was in control of. I'm deep in thought, driving without thought as we leave the parking lot of what used to be Roman's coffee shop. He died in the same place he tried to kill Jason and Elizabeth. I pray he doesn't come back as someone else.

I round the corner, taking a right to enter the main road and pass the front of the shop. The building is blazing now, and its structure will crumble soon. A woman's figure stands in front of the building, but I can't make out who it is.

We draw nearer and her features come into view. She's tall, wearing stilettos and a red dress. Her red hair, the same as mine, drapes down her shoulders. *Karen?*

Fire trucks came to a halt in front of the building, blocking my view of Karen. I say to myself in a low voice, "Was that her? Was that my mom?"

Lisa gave me directions to her home because I couldn't remember how to get there since the one time I'd been. I also can't think for myself. My world is one fat blur.

We arrived at Lisa's. Once inside, Jason walks Elizabeth to her room, placing her neatly in the bed and tucking her in. Jason returned to the living area with Lisa as she explained why she kept silent about Elizabeth's reincarnation.

I dragged my weak body into Elizabeth's room. Her computer monitors still lining the walls. All showcasing something different, just as they did the first time I visited.

SpillSecrets is displayed on one monitor. I logged out of Cory's account. Cory doesn't exist. I logged into mine. The messages chimed repeatedly, reminding me of what I've missed.

Typing...

KarenVolkov joined the chat...

Private chat with KarenVolkov...

KarenVolkov: Heather, whoever you are helping can't save you from me. My business will always come first. You'll pay for betraying the only person you have left. You died in that fire along with your dad. I'll be seeing you soon. -Mom.

Typing...

Blank message.

Acknowledgments continued

To my readers, thank you for investing the time into this book and supporting me. You guys are amazing and I wouldn't be much of an author without you.

To my friends, Diamond and Cheyanne, thank you for giving me pointers and feedback. As always, thank you for supporting my endeavors (no matter how crazy they are). Thank you for beta reading.

To my parents, thank you for everything. Without you, none of this would have been possible. I love you guys.

To Mama Kathy and my amazing Grandmother, Tina, thank you for beta reading and giving me feedback. I depend on you guys more than you know.

To Amber and Ivy, thank you for allowing me to gain experience that has helped me write this book. Also, thank you for the motivation. Thank you for believing in me.

To Lexi, thank you for being my work mom. You've taught and continue to teach me so much. No matter where I go in life, and I mean this, I will never forget you.

Last, but certainly not least, to Janay. Thank you for talking me out of writing another YA book. Thanks for advising me to focus on this one. You were right. It was a much better idea.